HOME TO TEXAS

FRANK RODERUS

WOLFPACK
PUBLISHING
— EST 2013 —

Published in the United States by Wolfpack Publishing

Wolfpack Publishing
6032 Wheat Penny Avenue
Las Vegas, NV 89122

wolfpackpublishing.com

Paperback ISBN: 978-1-64119-451-8
eBook ISBN: 978-1-64119-430-3

Library of Congress Control Number: 2018961063

Cover Illustration: "In A Stampede," by Frederic Remington, from *Ranch Life and the Hunting Trail: Illustrated by Frederic Remington* by Theodore Roosevelt (The Century Co., 1888), Courtesy Beinecke Library, Yale University

HOME TO TEXAS

CHAPTER 1

THE FELLOW OFFERED TO CARVE MY INITIALS ON THE SKIRT corners of the new saddle, but I grinned at him and shook my head. Shoot, he wouldn't hardly have had room enough. Wouldn't that have looked silly? A pretty saddle like that messed up with something like C. McC. McM. all over it. Standing for Charles McCown McMurty. Now there is a good German name for you, for a fact. So, my daddy always claimed, anyway, except I believe it is just possible that he was pulling my leg when he said it.

Not that I went into so much windy detail with the fellow at the saddle shop. I was too busy admiring that new rig. I couldn't hardly wait to get it strapped onto a stout, long legged horse so I could try it out on my way home.

I was feeling right tickled with myself just then and had decided to reward me with the best- looking deep seated, double rigged, basket weave carved saddle to be found in this railhead town.

Oh, it was a fine feeling all right. The way things were

going for me I was near to expecting some white-wing doves to come fluttering up from the south at any moment to light on my shoulder and begin to coo. It was just that kind of day. Here I was twenty-three years old and already the world was waiting to spread itself out at my feet.

I'd gone and done it, though. By golly I had. And I had the cash to prove it, right there in the belt under my shirt.

I'd had to figure it four separate times before I could believe it myself, but it was as true as ever a thing could be true. I'd bought 2,420 aged steers at $16 a head, payable this fall. Paid out of pocket $276 for foods and such stuff. Just paid off nine hands for two and a half months work at $30 the month. And had had to pay $5 to the graybeard who'd tended Lucas Wiley when he was hurt in a fall and had to be replaced along the way.

And just this morning I had received $22.25 per head for the 2,414 head of steers we had arrived with, losing only six head the whole way along. And one of those six given voluntarily to a band of flea-crawling Indians who looked like they were fixing to starve.

What it all meant was that I could darn well buy my saddle. I could go home, pay off the price of those steers and yet have—after my saddle— close to fourteen thousand dollars free, clear and all mine.

With that much money in his jeans a fellow could do almost anything in this world, including buy himself a piece of land all his own and maybe then go do some serious talking with Evelyn Stewart, who has the biggest eyes and the fairest skin of any girl I had ever seen. And at seventeen she was of an age to be thinking of such things. As for myself, I'd been looking forward to that discussion since she was fourteen and I noticed for the first time that she was going to be shaped like a girl directly and not so much like a thinner, shorter version of her brothers.

So, was I having me a good time this day? I should say I was.

The man got done with polishing my new saddle, and it did catch the light pretty. I paid him and swung it up to my shoulder and carried it out into the sunlight.

The sorrel gelding that had been my night horse the whole way up because of his sure-footedness was tied right out front. I pulled off the old hull my folks had given me when I turned sixteen and let it drop. I straightened the blanket and slapped that new saddle on and tightened her up and just had to stand there and admire the outfit for a minute. Mmmm, it was pretty.

I glanced around and was pleased to see that I was not the only one who liked what he saw.

There was a kid standing there at the side of the street, a tow-headed youngun about ten years and a thousand miles younger than me. He was bareheaded and shoed instead of booted and it was easy to see he'd rather have a wide-brimmed hat and pointed-toed boots and a revolver hung at his belt than most anything else in the world. Them and a job playing nursemaid to a bunch of hardheaded, wild-eyed, long-horned beeves.

I grinned at him and motioned him closer. He looked around to both sides and behind him and when he didn't see anyone else near he shuffled a few steps closer.

"Are you a rider, kid?"

He hesitated a moment and then poked his chin way out into the space between us. "I can handle anything with hair on it an' maybe some things without," he declared.

"Could you use an extra saddle?"

"What?"

"If you got a better one, say so. It won't hurt my feelings any. But I cain't ride more than one at a time. If you want this one, it's yours." I nudged my old hull with a toe.

"You serious, mister?" From his tone I would say he was wondering where I had hidden the joke.

"Sure, I'm serious." I turned and fiddled with my new stirrup leathers, adjusting them to what looked to be right. The kid had moved up closer by the time I turned back to him.

"Well?" I asked him.

His face changed from a long, bony, boy's face into a wad of teeth surrounded by freckles. "Shee-oot!" he said.

The kid dropped to his knees in the dust of the street and ran his fingers over the scraped and cut and work roughened leather of that old saddle. There's a lot of women could live out their lives and never be caressed that gentle nor with more affection.

I took the sorrel's reins and stepped up into my new saddle. My, but it felt awful good. I turned the sorrel and jogged him away, back toward our camp where the herd had been held until delivery. I was sixty, seventy yards away before I heard a yell behind me. I stood in the stirrups and turned to look.

The kid was standing beside his saddle and flinging both arms in the air. "Hey", he hollered. "Thanks."

I waved to him and went on.

The camp was a couple miles outside of town, and I drifted out there at a gentle lope that was mighty comfortable in that extra deep seated saddle. The cattle had been delivered and the boys paid off, but we still had a big remuda to hold. And Coosie's pack mules. We had hauled our stuff on mules to save the cost of buying and outfitting a cook wagon. It had worked out all right.

Jaimie Hunt was holding the remuda. More or less. It was a warm and pleasant day and those horses had had plenty of time to get used to the idea of staying together, so there wasn't much work to it. Most of the stock was dozing or nibbling lazily at the grass, and a few had flopped down and curled up like a pack of dogs soaking up sunshine after a hard night's run. Jaimie was slumped in his saddle, and his pony was standing hip-shot with its head down. The both of them looked to be asleep, but I knew if there was any commotion among the horses they would be Johnny-on-the-spot to head it off. Jaimie was seventeen and the youngest of the crew, but he was as dependable as any hand among us and turned in a day's work starting each and every sunrise.

Coosie had a fire going, for no special reason I knew of except that wherever he was there was always a fire lighted and ready for cooking or boiling coffee. He was perched close by it in the folding chair that was his special place. That chair was the first thing to be set up and the last thing loaded every move we made. It traveled atop the pack of his lead mule and was never touched by another soul the whole way north, me included. I don't doubt that I would have lost us a good cook if I'd ever tried to sit in it.

The Kraus brothers were hunkered down nearby, sipping at coffee and seeing could they get a rise out of Coosie while they bragged to each other on their mama's cooking and how much they were looking forward to having some of it again.

The Kraus boys were average height, about the same as me, but where I am built on the narrow side they were made thick and blocky and were terrible strong. I've never seen another pair that could best them for working on the ground at branding. They could flank, cut, earmark and brand just like a machine a-working and do it for as long as someone kept the calves and the irons flowing to them. They were close to two years apart in age but looked alike enough to be twins. For some reason their mama had named the both of them Theodore. To tell them apart they were called Theo and Teddy, Teddy being nineteen and the younger of the two.

I swung off the sorrel and tied him to a picket stake already stuck in the ground from where we'd been using them while we held the cattle near here the past few days. I have heard a lot of people talk about horses that will ground-rein and stay there until the boss says otherwise. About all I have to say on that subject is that I've heard it but never seen one of those fine animals, though I have personally seen several fellows walking back to camp. The most I have even seen myself is animals that have learned not to step on their own reins dragging on the ground.

Coosie and the Kraus boys nodded to me but never said one word about my new saddle even though it was gleaming in the sunshine like a shiny new coin. Well, I wasn't going to be the first to mention it either.

I drifted over near them and stretched and scratched for a minute, and the Kraus boys went back to talking about their mama's biscuits and gravy. Coosie was sitting quiet with his eyes drooping half closed and his hands folded across his belly.

"Got a piece of clean rag, Coosie?" I asked him.

With his eyes still mostly shut he grunted and said, "Sure." He left his chair and went to the pile of leather sacks he kept all his stuff in and dug into the correct one first time and came up with a bandanna sized piece of cloth. Those sacks, which hung on either side of the pack saddles when we were moving, were another thing nobody ever touched but Coosie. Jaimie had done it once, early on, and got whacked across the shoulders with a long-handled paddle, and all of us ate a gritty, half-cooked meal that night, which was the last time anyone messed with Coosie's sacks.

I took the rag and thanked him and went back to the sorrel. I rubbed and polished at that new saddle for quite a while and admired the smell of the new leather mixed in with the warm, good smell of healthy horseflesh. Still nobody said a word about that pretty saddle.

Finally, I gave it up and went back to the fire. I returned the rag to Coosie and right away he put it back where it belonged.

I plucked a tin mug off the string of them and poured myself some coffee. Among the good things I could say about Coosie is that a man could always find coffee at his fire, day or night and no matter the weather. He always put the pot on right away and somewhere close would make a rack of sticks or would string a thong from one picket stake to another, so he could hang a supply of cups ready to hand. Under that he would set a can of condensed milk and a jar of brown sugar. If it was raining he would set those into a pot with a wide lid, but they were always there.

I loaded my coffee with milk and sugar and squatted by the Kraus boys.

"Any excitement in town, Charlie?" Theo asked in an innocent tone of voice.

"Naw, nothing special." I sipped at the coffee and found it was good. "I could relieve Jaimie if you boys want to go look around a while."

"Aw, we aren't much for carousing," Teddy said. "We'll stay here an' save our money to carry home with us."

"Suit yourselves," I told them. "Are y'all in a hurry to get home?"

"Not a big hurry, but we figure to be heading that way," Theo said.

"I've got an idea if you're interested," I told them. They nodded and waited.

"The thing is, I'm getting itchy to be home quick as I can..."

"I would be too," Teddy said with a grin. I guess my intentions were no big secret.

"So, what I was thinking," I went on, ignoring him, "was that you boys and maybe one other could take the remuda down for me, and I could ride on ahead. I'll pay a month's wages for each." Theo looked at his brother and got a nod. "Sounds fair to me," he said. "You got a deal, Charlie."

"Good," I told them. "Go ahead and ask whoever else you want to go with you. I won't have to put up with whoever it is, so y'all choose for yourselves." I had a pretty good idea of who they'd want with them, though, and I figured to be satisfied.

"Mind if I borrow your sorrel a minute?" Teddy asked.

One of his string was staked out and saddled just as close but I never looked toward it. "Go ahead," I told him.

He took the sorrel and went out to wake Jaimie. They talked a minute or two and Teddy came back. He tied my sorrel back where it had been and hunkered down beside his brother again.

"That makes three," was all he said. Not a word about my saddle.

I stood and pulled my shirt out of my britches, so I could get at my money belt and gave Theo a hundred-dollar bill, which was about the only kind of bill I had in there. There wouldn't have been room for small stuff.

"That will cover the three of you and some left for food if you need any along the way, but you can take whatever you want from what we have leftover here."

He nodded and pocketed the bill.

The mules and pack saddles and sacks and most of the cooking gear belonged to Coosie, which was why he drew half again as much as a regular hand. It was amazing how in the few years since the long drives got started specialists like Coosie started showing up where there was work for them. You would have thought he'd been doing this all his life, but it could not have been more than four or five years tops.

Of course, he might have worked on some of those old-time drives to New Orleans or up into Illinois or Iowa, but it wasn't real likely. Those had been small herds of a few hundred head at a time going to a single slaughter house or feedlot or farmer and not well-organized drives like the coming of the railroads allowed.

"I'll leave in the morning then," I told the Kraus boys. "Y'all can head south whenever you want."

"We'll probably go then too, unless Jaimie wants to raise a little Ned first." He smiled. "If he does I'll hold onto his pay until we get home. You want the horses taken to your daddy's place?"

"Yeah. Drop them in the pens there. I'll sort them out however he wants them later."

"All right."

That was a load off my mind. I would've needed help getting the remuda home anyway. This way, I could get home a week or more earlier. And I was some anxious to be there.

I had it all figured out. I would borrow the folks' buggy and their team of matched blacks to go make my call at the Stewart place. We could take a drive out the river road to have that discussion. That would give Evelyn plenty of time to make up her mind. She was sure to know what I intended as quick as she saw me in a suit with a tie on and a fresh collar. She has always teased me because I don't like the feel of a hard collar up around my neck and generally will let one go limp before I will wear it, even to Services. Mama gave up fussing with me about that a long time ago, but Evie never had. That was the first thing she had ever joked with me about, and she still did it. Yes, I had it all thought out.

The rest of the boys drifted in and out that afternoon and evening except for Lee Miles and Bud Terry. Terry was the man we'd picked up three weeks south when Lucas had rode his pony one jump too many and got himself banged up. None of us knew this new man too well, though nearly everyone else of the crew had been around the same patch of southern Texas practically forever.

Anyway, Coosie fed everyone as they came and kept the coffee hot and said he would fix a good breakfast for any who had the stomach for it before he pulled out for wherever he was going next.

This had been a good crew and if I came north again the next year I was hoping I could get them together again, and I told them so.

I turned in early myself and listened to the chatter for the last time and thought about Evie and about the kind of range I'd like to locate for my own. Our own. It was some time before I could sleep.

CHAPTER 2

I PUSHED RIGHT ALONG THE NEXT DAY AND HAD MADE twenty miles before I stopped for nooning. I would not want to be doing that day after day. It would be hurtful to the horse. But for now, the sorrel was in fine shape and had had several days of loafing around until the cattle were sold. And I did have the excuse of being in a hurry to get home. Hereafter, though, I figured to pace it out to twenty-five or thirty miles to the day. Start late and stop early and let the horse graze long so as the keep him in good flesh. There could be no carrying enough grain to feed him for such a distance and time.

I had my bedroll and a sack of eatables tied on behind my saddle. When I stopped at mid-day I pulled the gear off the sorrel and hobbled him, so he could eat a bite and wallow if he wanted to dry the sweat where the saddle blanket had been.

There were plenty of dried cow patties along the wide-beaten beef trail, so I piled some together and made my fire with them. I was carrying some tin cans to do my cooking in. One of them I used to boil up some coffee. In the other I made a sort of a stew of beans and dried beef crumbled into the mess. It was not quality eating, but it would do, and simple stuff such as that was better than taking a lot of trouble over my meals.

Since I was making such good time I ate and then lazed by the fire with a second boiling of my coffee grounds. I had forgot to carry sugar or a can of milk, but I did not mind overmuch. It was too nice a day to worry about small things.

I was sitting with my belly full and my hat tipped forward over my eyes when I heard the approach of some quick-moving horses. I shoved my hat back and looked in time to see them veer my way. I stood and waved to them, and they pulled to a stop beside me.

"Hey, Lee. Bud. Get down and have some coffee an' let those horses rest."

They were all smiles. They got off their animals and ground-reined them, which was entirely their own business of course. The chestnut Lee was riding began to sidle away one short step at a time.

"I sure didn't expect to see you boys south of town fora while," I said. "I figured you'd be there as long as your pay held out."

"We were," Lee said. He helped himself to the last of the coffee.

Bud Terry got his canteen and spilled some fresh coffee beans into the can to make another batch of it.

"Do you mean to tell me that y'all managed to blow all your pay in one night?"

"Yeah, but it was some night, Charlie." Lee took his

hat off and rubbed at his head.

"It's a wonder you guys can sit on a horse this morning, much less take off at a run like you must've been doing. What's the big rush, anyway?"

Lee looked at Terry. He seemed nervous for some reason. He licked his lips and looked down toward his boot toes.

"Well you see, Charlie," he said. "We . . . that is, Bud and me ... we wanted to talk to you."

I shrugged. "Sure, Lee. What about?"

He looked at Terry again, but Terry did not seem to be in much of a mood for talking. Lee licked his lips again. "Well, Charlie... about money, it is."

"I don't follow you, Lee. I didn't short you on your pay or anything, I hope."

Lee shook his head quickly. "Naw, Charlie. You wouldn't have done a thing like that. But we... Bud and me ... we figure maybe you could let us have some more. I mean, we're broke . . . and you got quite a wad for them beeves."

"I guess I did, Lee, but, ah... I guess I could let you have ten. You can pay me back whenever you can or work it out next year. I'll likely take another herd north then, and I'd be proud to have you in the crew, Lee." I did not say the same to Terry. I didn't figure I owed him anything. Lee, though, was a down-home boy and was in need.

"That's real decent of you, Charlie," Lee said. But I noticed that he kept his eyes down when he said it.

"Something else, Lee?"

He started to speak but Bud Terry broke in. "What the kid means, McMurty, is that him an' me figure that money'd do us more good than it would you. We figure to have it all."

"When you put it plain like that, Bud, I guess I do understand," I told him. "You boys are fixing to go in for robbery."

I said the words, but they were just so many words coming out of my mouth. I really did not believe it. Not in the ways that count. I mean, here it was such a bright and pretty day and I had my belly full and a stout horse and Evelyn Stewart waiting to the south a few weeks' ride. And these weren't some unwashed, gun-toting strangers I was talking to. These were boys I had ridden with and shared coffee with and woke up for night herd watches.

Lee Miles had grown up in the same county as me. We'd been knowing each other for as long as I could remember. We had ridden together three or four times when bunches of us younger ones decided we were tired of border raiders hitting our beeves and we crossed the river to devil them and bring back any Texas-branded cattle we could find. He had been one of the quickest to call for justice when Spunky Watson was jailed in Matamoros and the Mexicans wouldn't let him go. We had got up a provisional company of sorts, complete with a bright red flag, and Lee had been for smoking the whole town until a frontier battalion of Rangers arranged for Spunky to escape and got things calmed down.

I looked at Lee and caught his eyes for a moment before he dropped them again, and I believe he knew I was remembering these things about him. I still could not believe that Lee Miles intended to rob me and to rob all those other people whose steers I had not yet paid for.

He knew who they were, too. He had helped gather the herd before we ever started them north those months before.

I heard a rolling click and looked to see what it was. Bud Terry had pulled the Remington .44 Army that he favored and had cocked it. It was pointed toward the ground about midway between us, but the threat was plain enough.

"You might as well shuck off that money belt, McMurty," he said.

"You figure it's going to be that easy, Bud?"

"Ayup. That or I blow five holes through you an' take it off your corpse," he said.

Lee looked at him and seemed somewhat irritated. "That ain't necessary. We agreed to that, Bud."

"He didn't," Terry said. He waved the muzzle of his pistol at me for emphasis.

"C'mon, Charlie," Lee said. His eyes were pleading with me although the tone of his voice was not. "There's no sense in making this any worse."

"You haven't gone so far that you can't back off, Lee. Y'all ride off now, and we'll forget the whole thing. I won't say a word to your folks nor to anyone else. I promise.".

Lee shook his head stubbornly. "I can't do that, Charlie. I've had it with bad horses and thorns and wild cattle. I'm not going back, and I'm not going away broke." He spread his hands and looked at me square. "It just isn't for me, Charlie. Not anymore." He got sort of a half-smile and said, "Anyway, you can make yourself another pile. This won't do more than slow you down some, but I'll never have another chance at such big money."

I still could not really believe it. Not standing there, face to face talking with them. And I could not believe that Lee was really willing to go back on all the friends he'd ever had.

"I'll make a deal with you then, Lee," I said, trying to think of a way to make it less. "You know who most of this belongs to. Take the part of it that's mine and leave the rest. I'll have to go home to deliver the price of our herd. That will give you about a month's start on me. That's the best I can do."

Bud Terry laughed out loud. I would like to believe that Lee might have gone for it. Those men down home were friends of his too. But Terry laughed and said, "You must be some kind of choir boy, McMurty. Now quit wasting our time and give us the belt."

Well, I was commencing to believe that it was really happening. I looked at Lee, and he shrugged.

"It's a fair proposition," I told him. I felt no inclination to reason with Bud Terry.

Lee shook his head no, and that seemed to be that.

As deliberately as if I was just going to take it out to look at it, I reached for my old Dragoon-style revolver. I had not been expecting trouble from men I had ridden with, so the safety thong was still over the hammer to keep the thing from falling out if the sorrel offered to buck. I knew I had no chance to use the gun.

And I did not.

I was still messing with the safety thong when Terry took a step to the side so Lee would not be in his line of fire. I was looking straight at him when he pulled the trigger. I could see it as plain as anything. A spout of fire better than a foot long. I felt something hit me in the body like a heavy- muscle blacksmith giving his hammer a full swing. I never did see his smoke or hear the shot.

The next thing I knew I was on the ground, though I do not remember falling. My eyes seemed to be shut. At least I could not see anything.

I heard boots shuffling around, coming closer.

"Do you think you killed him?" It was Lee's voice.

"I hope so. I don't wanta have to shoot him again." Terry's voice seemed unsteady. "I don't like shooting people. I swear I don't."

"I thought you used to be a soldier."

"That's different. You don't look at an enemy soldier as people. That ain't the same thing."

I heard the crunch of small stones under a boot sole and felt someone tugging at my shirt.

"The belt's all bloody," Lee said.

"Shut up about that," Terry snapped. "Take the thing an' let's get away from here. Somebody might have heard the shot."

"Not likely," Lee said.

I could feel something moving against my stomach and a scraping pull around my waistline. "Got it."

"It's about time. Come on now."

The boots moved away, and I heard someone curse.

"Where'd he get to?" Lee asked.

"Well, we ain't taking time to look. Take the sorrel. McMurty won't be needing it."

I heard them ride off and for a long time afterward heard nothing.

CHAPTER 3

I WOKE UP JUST BEFORE DAWN AS USUAL AND FELT A BIT chilly but not really uncomfortable. Coosie had not started the breakfast fire, and I was peeved with him. I went to roll out and do it myself, and the pain hit me. I cried out in the night.

For a long time, I lay on the ground with my legs drawn up toward my belly, but no amount of wishing would make this hurt go away. It felt like someone had packed my chest full of glowing red hardwood coals. Every heartbeat seemed to intensify the pain for just a flicker of a moment. I could feel every pulse-beat like a tiny bellows pumping onto those coals and making them that much worse.

The ball from Bud Terry's revolver had struck low in my rib cage to the right of center. Where it had gone and what it had done inside, I could not know. Perhaps it was better that I could not.

What I did know was how it felt, and that was worse than I could ever have imagined. I've had my share of wrecks with bad horses and once took a horn through the calf of my left leg while I was tending to business with a weanling bull calf on my right, but this was more than I ever knew or wanted to know before.

I lay there running sweat and racked by freezing chills at the same time, unable to move for fear it would get worse. The sun came up but did not do a thing to warm me.

After a time, I got tired of counting heartbeats and waiting to die. I opened my eyes and began to pay some attention to what was around me at this place.

There was little enough to see. The ashes of yesterday's noon fire were practically beside me, close enough that I was lucky I hadn't been burned too. Beyond that, maybe six feet away, was my food sack. The can I'd used for making coffee and that Bud Terry had refilled was on its side in the ashes, blackened now and empty.

Seeing that can got me to thinking of water. Lordy, but I was thirsty. My canteen had been by my saddle. I remembered stripping the gear off the sorrel and putting my new saddle down not too far from the fire.

I craned my head around at considerable expense in worse pain, but I could not see either the saddle or the canteen.

It came back to me that they had said something about taking my sorrel. They must have taken the saddle too. Probably Lee's ground-hitched animal had wandered off completely by the time they were done with their shooting and robbing.

I never would have believed that of Lee Miles. Never. We had never been best friends or anything like that, but we had run together considerable and I had thought of him as a friend. Well, I guess I knew better now.

That sort of thing was not pleasant to think about, but it was better in some ways than fretting about my lack of water. At least that miserable business with Lee Miles and Bud Terry was over and done with. My desire for water was a continuing and even a growing thing. The more I thought about it the worse it got, and I could think of no way to change a single part of that. As far as I knew there was no water closer than the Arkansas, and that was some miles away.

I stared and stared at the food sack lying beyond the dead ashes and tried to remember if I had thrown in any canned foods that might have been packed in juice that I could drink. I could not remember. A short twenty-four hours before, that sort of thing held no interest for me.

There was only one thing to do now, regardless. I had to crawl over there and look.

I lay still for a moment dreading it. I was running sweat all the more just from thinking about it. By itself, though, the worrying would not get it done. For that I had to move. I straightened my legs, slow and cautious.

That part did not hurt near as much as I expected. My legs were all right, of course. It was the lower part of my chest that had a hole blown through it.

I thought about rolling onto my stomach and moved my arms, about to do that. That was a mistake. That blacksmith was bouncing his tongs on my ribs. I cried out, and somehow that got me to coughing. Every heave of my chest was an agony of lancing fire in that wound.

I seemed to be cold and to be hot at the same time,

and I believe I may have been crying some. It seemed an awfully long time until the coughing died away. The regular level of pain in my chest was almost a relief in comparison. I lay still for a while until my breathing was under control.

It was time to try it again but this time I had some experience to guide me. I gritted my teeth and flopped over onto my back. The impact when my shoulders hit the ground was wicked, but at least I was prepared for it.

I rested for a moment, but it was easier now. That tiny bit of motion had given me a real feeling of accomplishment.

Using just my legs I dug my heels into the dirt and shoved myself around and toward the food sack. In no more than a month or two I reached it. I was worn out and panting by the time I did, the sheets of fire washing through my chest with every shuddering breath, but I had made it. I was feeling ridiculously proud of myself for having covered those few feet of ground.

I didn't try to roll over, just stayed the way I was and pulled the sack around to where I could dig into it. I found a small bag of ready-ground coffee beans and a whole mess of dried beans. There were quite a few tough, thin strips of jerked meat and one small, greasy chunk of bacon. Another small sack held a mixture of flour and salt and whatever else Coosie used in it so all I had to do was add water to make pan bread. Sure. All I had to do was add the water.

Not the first can of anything. No sweet, sticky syrup or acid, biting juices of any kind. Nothing but dry stuff that would be light for traveling. Hadn't I been a bright fellow?

For lack of anything better to do I took a few sticks of jerky and chewed on them. They would have tasted really good if they had not been so dry. As it was, well, they didn't do any harm anyway, and they did fill my stomach. I hadn't realized before that I had been hungry too, but I guess I was.

Not that this helped my thirst, but for a few minutes I was able to forget about that.

After I ate I lay for a very long time watching the sun climb and start to sink again. I spent most of that time wondering how long a man can last without water. I didn't know. South Texas is pretty dry at times, but it is no desert. You can always find a run of water somewhere not too far away, so it was not a thing I had given much thought to in the past. I understand there is some genuine desert to the west of us over in the northern states of Mexico and in our own western territories, but I had never seen any of those. Probably someone from there could have told me how many days or how many hours a man could survive with food but without water.

This was no desert here either. It was good grassland, fairly-well watered. Both ahead of me and behind I could find water in a half day's ride or less. If, that is, I was riding anywhere.

Shucks, I wouldn't even have worried, really, if I'd been afoot and had to walk to the next water. If I'd been otherwise healthy. A big if, that.

As things stood I just did not know. It would be quite a question whether I could get to my feet in the shape I was in, much less start out on a long, dry hike once I got myself upright.

I moved my arms a little to sort of test things out. I found out quick enough that I was not going marching this day. I felt like some Indian had crawled inside me and was using flaming torches to beat out the rhythm of a wild, savage dance on my ribs. I had to be pretty well messed up in there.

I spent the afternoon lying quiet, worrying, every so often forcing another piece of jerky down a dry throat. I did not really want to keep eating dry, flint-hard jerky, but I figured my only chance—poor as it was—would be to try to get some strength up and go for some walking.

I nibbled and dozed through the afternoon and finally fell into a dazed sleep that night, which was at least a form of relief from the thirst that was really beginning to torment me.

Morning found my tongue a little swollen and my lips and the inside of my mouth actually hurtful. There was no danger that it would surpass the hurt in my chest, not yet, but it was sure there and was growing.

There was one good point. The hole in my chest seemed to be not quite so bad this morning. Either it felt somewhat better or I was getting used to it, and I don't think a man could rightly get used to something like that.

I knew if I was ever going to move toward some water I would have to do it now or not at all. I tried to eat more jerky but could not do it. It hurt too much trying to chew so I spit it out, still as dry as when I had bit it off.

I rolled onto my left side, and the pain was nearly

enough to drive me onto my back again. It had not gone down so much after all.

It took a few minutes to get my breathing back to normal, but I had to go ahead. That or lay quiet and wait to die. I rolled the rest of the way over and got my arms under me. When I tried to push myself up it felt like everything inside my chest had been ripped loose, roots and all. I was dripping with sweat again, but I made it to my knees.

That was a mistake. What blood I had left drained out of my head. I was dizzy and felt as if I was reeling round and round even though I could feel the earth solid beneath my hands. My vision fogged red and swiftly went black altogether. I tried to reach forward—I think I was trying to steady myself, to grab something I could hold to —and fell heavily. I remember all too well the feeling when my chest slammed onto the ground.

The next thing I knew was a sound, low and soothing and homey. It came to me dimly the way sounds will carry through mist in the bayou country, seeming to come from all directions at once so you can hear something but not know where it is. This was a low sound and comforting, so very ordinary yet I could not remember what it was. I lay listening to it for a while, half aware of what I was doing, only half aware of my own being.

I remembered finally what the sound was. Cattle. It was cattle strung out in a big herd and being moved along the trail north. With them would be drovers, people who could help me. That knowledge brought me fully awake again.

I tried to lift my head, but I hadn't the strength to do

it. The best I could manage was to roll my head to the side.

My mouth was dry and felt like it had been packed with sand. I wanted desperately to call out to the men who would be riding flank this side of those animals. I tried to lick my lips. I would have done as much good with a rasp. I tried to call out to them. I sucked air deep into my lungs, ignoring the ragged, searing pain that came in with it. I tried to yell, expelling the air with all my force.

A feeble, whooshing croak was all that came out. I found there was still enough moisture in my body that I could weep from the frustration.

I listened to the cattle pass until all I could hear was a distant thread of sound off to the north.

I must have slept then or passed out. The next thing I knew was sound again but closer.

"Over here, Clete. Hey! Over here."

I heard the creak of saddle leather and the sound of another horse approaching at a run.

"I'll bring the wagon," a second voice said.

I felt a hand touch my shoulder. I wanted to laugh and to shout but again a brief croak was all I could manage.

That was all right. Whoever it was knew I was alive. That was enough.

CHAPTER 4

"Man, oh man. This time yesterday you looked like we'd be putting you in the ground before this. That's the natural truth, McMurty. But I guess if you ain't died by now you won't. Not for a while anyhow."

The fellow was a lanky, easy talking old boy named Cletus Reed. He was taking a herd up from central Texas. Twenty-seven hundred aged beeves including culled stockers and a real handful to manage if the condition of their remuda was anything to judge by. Practically every horse there was purely worn out. But him and his crew had them headed north and no one was complaining.

What happened, Clete told me, was that one of his point men found Lee's chestnut, still saddled, wandering loose, so they took a swing around to see if they could find an embarrassed cowhand walking somewhere close. What they found, of course, was me.

A youngun named Randy Howard had done the actual finding, and Clete had done a hurry-up job of patching. They put me in their cook wagon atop all the bedrolls owned by the crew. It was better than I had any right to expect and I surely was grateful to Clete and his crew.

"There were times I got to wondering myself," I told him. "I wouldn't have made it much longer."

"Well, we'll carry you along with us to town. Oughta get there some time this evening or early tomorrow morning. You can get a proper doc to bind you up then, an' you can get away from the jostling of that wagon."

"That'll be some relief," I admitted with a grin. I could afford to do some grinning now.

Clete drifted off to join his crew in stringing the herd out after their nooning. They would move them for another couple hours and then stop pushing. That way the beeves would graze along a little while longer and come to an early stop of their own accord and fill their bellies. Brought along slow like that they would not lose any weight from traveling and depending on the grass might even gain some. It took longer than pressing them for speed, but you got a better price at the end of it. The commission men bought by the head but sold by the hundredweight and were generally willing to pay more for the heavier animals.

In a few minutes the cook—name of Coosie, too, but not the same fellow who'd been with us, of course—climbed onto the box of his wagon. Heavy loaded though it was, that wagon creaked and tilted when that big'un hefted himself aboard. He took up the reins and put a little pressure on and the team started off at a nice trot, pulling steady and even. They had been together a while.

Inside the wagon things were not so steady, though. Lying down in a moving wagon is a rugged proposition at the best of times, and with a hole in your chest you tend to notice the bumps and the bounces, each and every one. I tried bracing myself against the shocks, and I tried staying loose and limp. What I discovered was that I wasn't going to be comfortable regardless, and that was that.

I had already found out that their Coosie was not much of a talker so to take my thoughts off the wagon ride I opened the sack and other stuff they had laid in beside me—my own sack and the bedroll and saddle bags that had been on Lee's saddle, and which they naturally had figured was my gear.

The sack held my food and coffee and my gun belt with the Dragoon still there, nested in the coiled belt leather. I was surprised Lee and Bud Terry had not taken it. But I was pleased to find it there. I did figure to have need of it.

I put the gun back in the sack and laid that aside. The bedroll was not as good as my own had been. Mine had been an extra heavy soogan stuffed and quilted for me by my mother and wrapped in a tarp. Lee's bedroll was a pair of wool blankets rolled up into an old slicker too torn to wear. I laid that aside—it would do—and pulled the saddle bags to me.

Lee had not carried a heck of a lot with him: One spare shirt, which I needed as a replacement for the hole-punched and blood-caked thing I was still wearing. A pair of socks, which needed washing. His dress-up spurs, which had brass Lone Stars inlaid on them. A handful of

.44 caliber balls, which I could use in my Dragoon, but no mold to make more. A flask mostly full of gunpowder. And a tin of percussion caps. That was it.

While I was at it I checked my pockets, too. Twenty-seven dollars in coin and a folding knife. Apparently, they hadn't taken time to go through my pockets either.

Twenty-seven dollars. It would have to do, but it sure was a long way from the more than fifty-two thousand those boys had lifted off me.

Anyway, Cletus Reed and his crew carried me back into town and found a doctor for me. That gentleman looked me over and said "humph" and "hmmm" several times and finally accused Cletus of doing him out of a fee.

"The truth is, Mr. McMurty, that these gentlemen have already bound the opening. You remain alive. The puncture shows no inclination to fester. The recuperative process may now proceed at its own pace. All you can do is rest and wait patiently."

"Do you think it'll take long, Doc?"

He shrugged with exaggerated eloquence. "Who can say? You have a broken rib and a deep puncture. In all probability there was damage to a lobe of your lung. I observe a shortness of breath as you speak, you see. Also, the projectile itself remains lodged within the chest cavity. I am sure you noticed there was no exit wound. However, I would not advise probing for the bullet. That would aggravate the wound perhaps more than the bene-fits would justify." He smiled. "This way you may be able to awe your grandchildren with stories of the lead ball in your chest."

The good doctor had refrained from asking any questions about how I came to be in that condition, nor did he then take the opportunity I thought he was making for himself. Perhaps he simply did not care. Either that or his job had given him an extraordinary amount of control over whatever natural curiosity he possessed.

I thanked him, and Cletus clucked the team ahead.

"Where to?" Reed asked.

"Good grief. I haven't any idea," I told him.

I had not thought about that before, but I had nowhere to go. And I hadn't enough money to put up in a hotel for any extended period. "Maybe... maybe some of my crew are still in town or something. One of them might have some ideas."

Cletus Reed was being awfully patient with me, and me a complete stranger. "Aw, we'll take you on back to our camp," Reed said. "It'll take a couple days for us to make our deal and get the herd delivered. Maybe that will give you some breathing room."

What can you say to something like that except "yes" and "thank you"?

We jostled and jounced back out of town, and I was quite glad when we got back to Reed's herd and Coosie unhitched his team. Because of me the crew would have to eat their night meal way late, but not a one of them was complaining and each had a cheerful word for me. This was a good bunch. Not any better than my own boys, of course. Except two.

While Coosie got some steaks burning, the hands lifted me out of the wagon and got me set up on Lee's bedroll with his saddle—about as scraped and rough looking as my old one had been—tucked behind my neck and shoulders. That was awfully nice of them. It also let them get to their own bedrolls, which I had been lying on all day.

The next day the wagon stayed in place near the fire and the always-hot pot of coffee. Coosie and a couple of the boys—I found out one of them was related to the Kraus boys' mother— rigged a tarp out from the wagon bows and hauled me under it so I would be shaded from the sun.

It had been four days now and I was not exactly up to running around the camp or leaping onto a horse. The only improvement I could notice was that the fire might have been banked, like for a long, slow burn. Now it was more of a deep, dull, constant pain. It sure was a good one, though. It seemed to fill my whole chest, and whenever I was moved I could still feel every heartbeat like a blow from a small, insistent hammer. Still, I was awfully lucky. Bud Terry thought he had killed me, and he very nearly had.

I stayed under the tarp the whole morning with Coosie thoughtful about bringing more coffee whenever I wanted it. After dinner a buggy came rattling past and took a turn around the herd. A little while later it pulled to a stop near the fire with Cletus riding alongside.

The buyer who got out was all smiles and it was easy to see they had made a deal, for Cletus was grinning too.

The buyer was Dean Shoup, the same man who'd made the best offer for my herd just the week before. He seemed to be doing all right for himself, and I hoped he was. The better he did, the better we could expect to do in our turn.

Shoup seemed right taken aback when he saw me. He took the cup of coffee Coosie handed him and brought it under my tarp.

"Charlie? Charlie McMurty. Whatever happened? Are you all right?"

I grinned at him. "Compared to what, Mr. Shoup?"

"He looks a sight better than when we found him a couple days ago," Clete said.

"What happened?"

"There was some argument about who should get to use that money you paid me. I seem to have lost."

"Got himself shot is what happened, Mr. Shoup."

The commission man seemed genuinely upset. "Mr. McMurty, I assure you I said nothing to anyone about our transaction. I didn't even know your plans. I hope you don't think…"

"Of course not, Mr. Shoup. I wouldn't have let strangers get me in such a fix. No sir, these were friends of mine." I laughed and felt the fires in my chest rekindle.

"You Texans have strange friendships then," Shoup said.

"Yeah, well, I guess everyone makes a mistake now and again."

"Rather costly, I would say."

"Not half as bad as it might have been, though."

"He was close to cashing in when we found him," Clete said, "but Texas boys come tough even if we are stupid at times."

"I'm really sorry about this, McMurty. If there is anything I can do..." He let his voice trail away.

"Thank you, Mr. Shoup, but I don't... Now wait a minute. Maybe there is a way you could help me. If it wouldn't be too much of a bother, that is."

"Name it."

"Well, sir. Last week you mentioned that you spend so much time here you've rented a house."

"Yes, I have. I don't care for hotels. Quite a nuisance in my line of work, that is, too."

"The thing is, Mr. Reed and his crew have been mighty generous about letting me lie around underfoot, but in a few days, they'll be heading home. It will be a while before I can ride again, and..."

"And you need a place to stay while you heal," he broke in voluntarily. "There is a spare bedroom in my house, and of course you shall use it. It will be good to have your company."

"To tell you the truth, Mr. Shoup, that is exactly what I was hoping you would say. And I thank you most kindly."

"Do you think you could manage in my buggy, McMurty?"

"I'll give it a whirl," I told him.

Cletus Reed eyed the light vehicle skeptically. It was a two-seater with only a luggage boot behind the padded and upholstered bench. He said, "Our wagon has room for stretching out. It'd be better, I b'lieve. Be glad to bring him in in that tomorrow morning."

"Would that be' all right with you, McMurty?"

"Yes sir, it sure would be."

"Good," Shoup said. He turned to Clete. "I'll see you both in town tomorrow then, and I'll have a binder payment ready for you then, Mr. Reed. The balance will be available to you as soon as the herd is tallied on delivery."

They shook on it, and Shoup nodded his good-byes.

CHAPTER 5

THE HOUSE SHOUP HAD RENTED WAS SMALL BUT comfortable. It was kept tidy by a middle-aged Danish lady named Hedriksen. Her husband worked for the railroad in some capacity that I never did get straight. I don't know when she ever found the time to do anything for him. She arrived ready for work promptly at seven each morning and did not leave until after the evening meal was cooked, eaten and cleaned up after.

Mrs. Hedriksen had the devil's own time with the English language and perhaps because of that or perhaps because of a natural reticence she almost never spoke. Whatever, that did not keep her from staying busy. She was not an especially warm or motherly sort of person, but she was almighty busy. From my small room at the back of the house I could hear a constant clatter and scrape and shuffle as she cooked or scrubbed or dusted or ironed or mended.

As for the extra burden I placed on her, I could see neither resentment nor interest and I doubt that Shoup could either. She carried huge meals in to me at the hours appointed by Shoup. She carried the trays out again without comment. Twice a day she emptied, cleaned and returned the crockery slop jar that had been placed beside my bed. Once daily she changed my bed linen, which was a real wonder for she did it with me still in the bed, doing the job by halves and shuffling me from side to side so she could have room to work. The clean linen was always freshly ironed and smelled and felt wonderful.

Shoup was a busy one himself at this time of year, spending most of his time among the arriving herds or at the loading pens or setting up drinks for the trail bosses who had not yet struck a contract for their beeves. He also spent a good deal of time in the telegraph and railroad offices arranging transport and sales of the animals he bought here and shipped back east to the stockyards or wherever.

The result of all this was that I spent a quiet and even sort of lonesome week until I felt well enough that I could get off the bed and move around a little. Even then I had to go slow and easy, tottering from one hand support to the next. Wouldn't the boys at home have loved to put me on a rank horse in that condition? I'd have come unstuck after the first jump.

Even so it was quite a relief to be outside the house again. With a few days practice I could get to anywhere in town, although it took a while to do it, and I took to hanging out around the loading pens. I didn't see anyone I knew, but one bristly-faced fellow from Live Oak County said he would carry a letter south and see that it got to my folks. In it I explained where I was and some-thing of what had happened. I could not bring myself to tell them that Lee Miles was one of them. Mostly I was anxious for my folks to get the word around to those ranchers who had trusted me to pay them this fall for steers already driven away and sold at a profit. I did not want those men thinking I had been false with them.

It was some kind of a load off my mind to get that letter sent. In another month or so the Kraus boys and Jaimie Hunt would be showing up with the horse herd and with the word that I had been riding way ahead of them. If I wasn't home by then some people would have been starting to worry. And I was pretty sure at this point that I would not be home that soon. It was beginning to look like it would be a while before I saw Evelyn again.

One thing I was determined of. I was not going back until I got back at least the $38,7201 owed on those steers. No matter how far I had to go to find Lee Miles and Bud Terry. No matter what I had to do once I found them.

Once I was back on my feet I seemed to get better faster. Not much faster, but some, anyway. At least I got so I could walk without the jolt of each footfall tearing my chest apart—so long as I took it slow and easy. Mostly the problem was that I had no wind. Even a short walk got me to puffing and blowing like I'd been runner-up in a Fourth of July foot race.

As soon as I could make it that far and stay upright for a long enough time I got to looking around at the loading pens to see if there wasn't some way I could help Dean Shoup with his business there. I was getting some-what worried about being such a burden to the man, and him not owing me a thing nor hardly knowing me. What I finally came up with that he would agree to after some argument was for me to tally beeves onto the railroad cars for him at loading time and—much more important —to handle the tally by brand when he took delivery of a herd. Either one I could do sitting down.

Counting beeves into the cars was nothing more than counting them one-two-three as they went up the chute, and most any nitwit can do that, me included.

Working a brand book is something else again, and there you want to be careful. A mistake on the brand book can become a matter of real touchy lawing, with the inspector of brands for the county or state or whatever having the authority to make arrests and impound animals and pretty much whatever else they need to keep straight the ownership of animals moving through different states for sale and slaughter. The brand count you start with has to be the same one you end with, save for any losses, as a means to stop people from picking up replacements as they travel. Here the locals did not care overmuch whose beeves were sold as long as the drovers bringing them lingered to spend their pay, but the state of Texas and several individual counties had sent brand inspectors to keep an eye on things and there were reps from a number of different stockmen's associations as well. In all it made for a fair handful of people who were interested in proving their worth to whoever hired them, and Shoup was wanting to keep those counts correct down to the last head. Which I believe he would have done anyway, as he was a genuinely honorable man.

Anyway, I had been around cattle and reading brands

since I was big enough to know boo from hoo and so I could catch them quick as the beeves were strung out and trotted past Shoup's buggy. Accuracy was what you had to have there, but speed was a nice thing too as anyone can tell you who has had to take a separate and individual look at each animal in a herd of two to three thousand before the delivery is made formal and complete. One missed brand, though, in that moving stream of horns and hides can make for an awful lot of confusion, for you do not just shut off the movement of several hundred cattle the way you would shut the damper of a flue.

I remember one-time down home when old Mr. B. Williams was selling a herd of mixed yearlings and two-year-olds and the county man was there with his brand book trying to keep track of the seven or eight different brands the old gentleman had accumulated over the years.

The fellow making the tally was a bit slow anyway and already had everyone's temper ready to blow from making them re-cut and re-list too many head. He did it one time too many and a fed-up waddie named Chaw Curtis, who always had a chaw stuffed in his cheek, got so mad he threw his hat down. Well, that did it. Something about Chaw's hat boogered the calves nearest him and that spread to the rest of them and pretty soon we had the dust boiling and tails streaming out in the wind for all directions. Those calves scattered like a bunch of quail.

The tally man, whose name I remember quite well but will not tell for he is really a nice fellow, looked up and watched all this commotion until those calves were near out of sight. Then he tipped his hat to Mr. B.

Williams and quietly walked his horse off toward home without saying a word to anyone more that day. Us younger fellows thought it such good sport we did not even mind the work of catching all those calves again, and Chaw is still asked about the well-being of his hat from time to time.

Anyway, it seemed to be a help to Mr. Shoup for me to handle that chore for him, and I felt a little less useless whenever there was such to be done, and it was something that could be handled from the buggy as easy as from horseback.

For going any real distance, I had to settle for the buggy for weeks and weeks, but I was getting there just the same. In about a month I could walk more or less normally save for a shortness of breath that just kept hanging on.

I still had more time on my hands than was comfortable, though, and I hadn't either the finances or the inclination to spend it drinking. I would have spent it trying to get information from people who'd come from any direction other than south—I needed to get a line on which way Lee Miles and Bud Terry might have gone—but just about everyone had come up from Texas to get here and would be headed back that way when they finished their business. And I knew Lee and Bud would not be going that way, for certain sure.

The next best thing I could think of for getting ready for what might be ahead was to make myself a whole lot more familiar with that old Dragoon I had been hauling around on my leg the last four or five years.

Like anyone else would do, I had shot the thing a

good bit when I first got it and then less after a while and now not at all for a long time. And I'd never really paid that much attention to the thing once I got used to having the weight there. It became no more than another common article like a hat or spurs or bandanna, something worn out of habit that might be used on a given day but probably wouldn't be.

The thing is, practically every male I know over the age of, say, seventeen wears a gun most every day, but I had never known a single one who fancied himself as being a pistolero. Neither me nor anyone else I knew really bothered all that much on the subject, Lee Miles not excepted. Guns really are more for making noise with than anything else and in a rare emergency come in handy for putting a ball through the horn of a particularly rank beef—and will that ever slow them down when they are feeling feisty—or maybe for dropping a bad one if you should be caught afoot by a bull or an overprotective mama cow.

With a couple dollars of what they had left on me I bought two pounds of fine grain powder, a sack of ready-made .44 caliber balls and another tin of caps, and I was ready to do some practicing.

There was a low bank along the railroad right of way east of town a quarter mile and I took to walking out there in the afternoons. At first, I just popped away at rocks and clods, to get my eye back, but what I would need in the future would be speed. I was going to have to learn how to get my gun to working in a hurry, without any warning ahead of time.

It saddened me to think that if I had done this same

thing before I brought the herd north, things might have been different. I could have fought Bud Terry instead of fumbling around with a scrap of rawhide while I watched him shoot me. And I honestly think if I'd done that I could have sent Lee riding and get the whole thing ended then and there.

But of course, it wasn't that way at all.

I found out pretty quickly just how impractical the average holster is. It gives you a place to carry a gun, protects it from being scratched and beat by brush and keeps it from falling out when your horse is in a storm of bucking and jumping. What it does not do is make it easy for you to get the gun in action when you need it, what with the gun being tied down into a deep pouch that can wander all around on a man's belt.

After giving the subject some thought I copied the army way of securing the holster high and forward for a draw across the body. That way it was always in the same place, whether I was mounted or afoot. Then I used my knife to whittle away the leather at the top, so I could grab the whole butt and hammer at one time instead of having to fish the Dragoon out of a pouch before I could get a good hold on it. And finally, I threw away that retaining thong. I wasn't going to get hung up on that a second time.

Then it was just a matter of plain old time-consuming practice. Pull-and-cock-till-your- arm-hurts practice. You wouldn't think that three pounds of metal and wood could feel so heavy, but it can. I pulled and cocked and pointed and dry-fired that old gun for weeks and broke a mainspring and two nipples doing it, but by the end of that time I could shuck that Dragoon and make it go click at the bat of an eye.

I got so I would not tell myself when to draw and snap but would wander around trying to stay loose and easy. Whenever a jackrabbit bounced or a bird fluttered, or a grasshopper jumped I would throw down on it, and after a time it got to be almost an unconscious reaction. I loaded her up and tried it with live ammunition for another week. When I found I could dust a jack when it paused at the end of its first leap I figured I was ready.

The thing was, though, that I still did not know if I would have the plain guts to do that same thing when there would be a man in front of me. It is one thing to shoot a deer or a jackrabbit. But a human life is another thing entirely. I knew now that I could take a bullet. I didn't think that would bother me if the time came for it again. I knew I could stand there and take it if I had to. The thing was, I did not know if I could deliver a bullet.

CHAPTER 6

I DID NOT REALLY KNOW THE CHESTNUT GELDING I HAD sort of inherited from Lee Miles, but he looked like a decent sort of animal, leggy and deep chested. He stood about 15-3 which is bigger than I generally like as usually a horse that tall does not have the cat quickness it takes to work the rough cattle. Still, with that much leg and that much chest he should make a fair animal for the far traveling I would be doing.

The horse had not been used in quite a while, spending the whole time of my recovery in a public livery courtesy of Mr. Shoup's generosity. When the saddle hit his back again he pinned his ears back and tried to side-step away until I settled him down with a quick snatch of the reins and a harsh word. He stood for me then but did not like it, keeping his ears back and his eyes wide.

He was going to be a handful when I mounted. I knew that and was not looking forward to it. I was pretty well healed now but I really did not want to go to fighting a rank horse just yet.

The hostler was a man I had talked with a few times during the weeks past, and he knew something of my troubles. He watched me tug the cinches tight before he stepped closer.

"There's generally some kids hanging around outside," he said. "I could get one o' them to ride this fella down a mite before you step onto him. He looks like he might be frisky."

I'd never done such a thing as to ask anyone else to do my riding, but the circumstances now were a bit unusual.

"Would it cost much?" I asked the gallused, bare-headed livery man.

He shrugged. "A quarter prob'ly. I could put it on Mr. Shoup's bill if you don't have it. Don't reckon he'd mind."

"Good Lord, no. I feel like a leech as it is, that man has already been so kind to me. No sir, I've got a couple dollars yet. I guess I'd best spend some of it that way."

The man nodded and went outside. I led the chestnut out of the barn to a stout corral out back. In a few minutes the hostler was back with a skinny, tow-headed kid.

The man aimed a thumb at the boy and said, "He'll do it."

"Can you ride, boy?"

The kid grinned. "Anything with hair on it. I told you that once before, mister."

"You did? Oh, yeah. I remember now. You sure did. Well, now you can show me." It was the boy I'd given my old saddle to. My, but that seemed a long time ago now.

"You bet," he said happily. He took the chestnut from me and hauled the animal's nose around to the stirrup until he got set in the saddle. When he let the horse have its head it snorted and flared its nostrils. It stood spraddle-legged and defiant for a minute. The boy thumped its ribs with his heels and the show began.

Turned out that old horse'd had quite a few kinks in its spine, but the boy was able to work them out. The chestnut reared and twisted and set up for some real high-flying, stiff-legged, plain and fancy bucking, but the boy stayed with him, all the while grinning and laughing like he was having the time of his young life. Which maybe he was, at that.

When the horse agreed to admit he was going to have to go back to being domesticated the dust settled back onto the ground again and the boy was right there, reining him through some tight figure eights to supple the beast's neck for me and get it used to rein and bit pressure again. Myself, I ride more with weight and spur than with the hands, but that is a habit you pick up when you are working on a horse instead of just riding it. The kid looked proud as a pup, and I guess he had a right to be. He brought the gelding back and stepped off beside me.

"That should calm 'im down, Mr. McMurty," the kid said.

"You did a nice job with him, too. How much do I owe you?"

The boy shook his head. "You already paid it." He grinned. "Besides, it was fun."

"You'll accept a thank-you, won't you?"

"Yes sir, I sure will." He gave me the reins and went off with a wave and a swagger. I hadn't noticed before but there was a gaggle of his buddies clustered at the corner of the livery where they had been watching the whole thing. The kid was getting some big-eyed admiration from the crowd over there, and I guess his day was made. I was glad for him for sure.

I thanked the hostler for his help and swung onto the now easy tempered chestnut. My, but it did feel good to have my legs wrapped around a horse again. The hostler swung the gate open, and I headed down the road.

The big question ahead of me now was which way I ought to go to start my looking. Any direction I chose was a gamble, of course, but I had given it considerable thought in the weeks past.

About the only thing I could be sure of was that Lee Miles and Bud Terry would not have gone back south into Texas. But they might have gone anywhere else, from California on east to New York or whatever. The only thing I had to go on was knowing that they were both, at the heart of things, cowhands. I was willing to bet they would stay in the grazing country somewhere, and it seemed to me that the territories west of the Pecos River had a reputation for harboring bad men who had money to spend. For no reason better than that I decided New Mexico or Arizona might be the best places to start looking.

The old Santa Fe trail was to the north of me, so I pointed the chestnut away from Texas and moved him on. It took a full day to reach it, but I had no trouble recognizing the trail when I got there. Fifty years of steady use had carved the wheel ruts deep and wide. The railroads were already building in that direction and in a few years would probably wipe out the old trail, at least so far as the heavy freighting would be concerned, but for now it was my best bet. I sure had never expected to be traveling this road, though.

I was still at my breakfast fire the next morning when I heard the rumble of wagons approaching. They came into sight over a low rise and rolled toward me, one after another until it seemed they would never end. In all there were more than twenty heavy rigs, each of them a wagon with man-high wheels coupled to a trailer nearly as big. Each rig was pulled by a dozen mules. Those were fine mules, too. Not your little Spanish cross like you find down home but the stout, heavy bodied animals they breed out of draft mares over in Missouri. As they came near an outrider at the front of the train pulled aside and moved my way.

He was a thick-bodied man with a full, dark beard and a floppy black hat that sagged around his ears. The effect made his face look like a nose and pair of eyes set amongst a patch of black fur. He looked me over carefully before he spoke a greeting.

"Hello, your own self," I told him. "Want some coffee?"

"Sure." He stepped off his horse and let the reins drop. He squatted by the fire and helped himself to the last that was in the can, using a mug of his own that he carried in a saddle bag. He tasted it and nodded his approval before he spoke again. "John Haven thanks you, sonny," he said. He probably was not ten years older than myself.

"I guess you're welcome, but I'd just as soon be called by my name," I said and told him what it was.

"All right," he agreed. "You traveling east?"

"No. Toward Santa Fe. Rumor has it this trail leads there."

"That just goes to show you that rumors can sometimes be truthful, and I should know. I been crossing this way twice a year since I was a pup. Traveling alone, are you?"

"You are awful mindful of my private business, John Haven."

"No offense intended," he said in a mild tone. "Not at all. It is just that I know what I am about on this trail and would offer some advice if you want to listen." He sipped at his coffee.

"In that case I guess I will listen to you."

"What I would say is this: Once you leave the protection of Fort Dodge traveling west you are in empty territory 'til you hit the Spanish settlements. You might ride on through and never see an Injun. You might find some and be greeted like a brother. Or you might find some an' become dead. Even a blanket Injun will lift a scalp sometimes if there is no one around to see it happen. My advice to you, Mr. McMurty, is to ride in the company of a freight train. It would be safer, I assure you."

"It's kind of you to think of my safety, Mr. Haven, but that would be a slow way to travel. My food would run out long before I could reach Santa Fe."

He smiled and his eyes, bright blue they were, danced. "Now I was hoping you would say something of the kind, Mr. McMurty, for I have a proposition to put you."

"Have you had this in mind all along, Mr. Haven?"

"Ever since I saw that rope on your saddle," he admitted. "I take it you have experience with the handling of livestock?"

"I have."

"Exactly," he said. "So, you see how nicely this works out. My night herder was a lad from Independence who became homesick for his mama several days ago. He departed, and now I have need of a herder."

"And in exchange I would have the protection of your company?" I asked without enthusiasm.

"That plus a breakfast for your supper, a supper for your breakfast, a bed in a wagon during the day. And forty dollars in hard money at the end of the journey."

Well, I had to consider it. He was probably right about the protection. There was still raiding going on away from the towns. And I could use forty dollars for sure.

"You have yourself a nighthawk, Mr. Haven," I told him.

"Nighthawk?"

"A mule herder if you prefer."

"Good." He offered his hand, and we shook on it. "Then I suggest we pack you up and go find your bed, for you will be working tonight."

It took only minutes for me to be loaded and ready while Haven kicked the fire apart. We rode forward along the line of freight wagons while he seemed to be lost in thought. When we reached the fourth from the front he bobbed his head as if to himself and said, "This one, I think, should be right for you, and the crew won't bother you." Haven let out a long, quavering yell and the whole train came to a halt. He was for sure the boss around here. He dismounted and told me, "Put your saddle in that trailer and tie the horse to it."

I did so and walked forward to meet the driver and his chore boy. Haven was standing on the ground below the tall, wide box that held a spring seat that was piled with pillows with faded red covers.

"Charles McMurty, this is Fritz Deutsch and his son Kurt. Don't worry about it if they don't talk to you very much. It won't be anything personal." They greeted me in German, which I recognized easily enough even if I don't speak it. There are a good many German settlements in parts of Texas, and I had heard it before. Both father and son, the one looking to be in his forties and the boy about fifteen, were red faced and as round as a pair of those potato and bread dumplings their womenfolk make, but there was plenty of muscle in them. They were not at all soft.

Their greeting sounded polite, whatever it was they said, and the father pointed a thumb toward the interior of the big wagon. I thanked him and Haven both and walked to the back of the wagon.

I threw my bedroll over the tailgate and climbed the short ladder that was bolted to the back end of the wagon. This wagon had a tight-fitting canvas cover although some of the freighters were completely open to sun and rain. When I got inside I could see why this one was covered. The floor of the freight box was filled with bales of yard goods wound onto flat bolts and bundled together. There was cloth of just about every color and description. No wonder Haven had said it would make a good bed wagon.

No sooner had I got inside than John Haven hollered again. Immediately there was a loud creak of harness leather and jangle of chain as twenty-some teams of mules laid into their collars and got the wheels to turning.

I was not tired, having woke up not more than an hour earlier, but I figured I might as well enjoy a life of ease and comfort while I could. I pulled my boots and trousers off and stretched out on the bales of cloth. The sway and the muffled jolts of the wagon were not at all uncomfortable.

CHAPTER 7

WE PASSED FORT LARNED FOUR DAYS LATER AND HEADED on toward Fort Dodge without bothering to stop. Apparently, there was nothing there of interest to John Haven except the enticements that might interfere with his muleskinner' work, and he was a man who liked to keep control of the things and the people around him.

It was no trick for me to adjust to the herding of a few hundred mules after handling scatter-brained beeves for so long. After a full day of work—and that was what Haven gave them—those mules were interested in grazing and dozing. They were not likely to take off on their own, and as far east as we still were it was unlikely that the herd would be raided by any of the roaming Indian tribes although I kept an eye out just the same.

During the night I swapped off the use of my own horse, Haven's and a mare belonging to his segundo, a man named Eric Fortunada who rode drag during the day. That way each animal had most of the night to do its eating and sleeping in.

The wagon crews were divided into four-wagon, eight-man messes with the cooking chores going from wagon to wagon by rotation, although as nighthawk I was not part of the cooking roster as I would be working while breakfast was being fixed and sleeping the rest of the time. Which was a good thing for the eight other men in the mess. I took my meals with the Deutsches, who turned out to be always even-tempered and agreeable even if I could not understand what they were saying most of the time, including when they spoke English, and with the men from the first three wagons of the train.

I would have expected a good many of the men freighting to Santa Fe to be Mexicans but at least in this train they were not. There was only one Mexican crew, and they were in a different mess. Most of the men were heavy built, rough dressed, rough talking men who seemed to think at about the same speed their wagons moved, which was not very fast. At meal times they seemed to think it interesting to tell each other how many rabbits they had seen lately or if their near wheeler had worked up a good sweat, and in the evening, they retold the same things and then went to bed. They were not ones for singing or gambling or such amusements as you might find around a cow camp. I could not say that I felt close to any of them, but neither did I have any real trouble with any of them.

One thing I noticed that seemed awfully odd and that was that every so often a couple of them would get into a fight with their fists. You will not likely find much fighting among cowhands but when you do it is going to be with a gun or maybe a knife. These fellows did not seem to mind the idea of battering their own hands all puffed and bloody against the other guy's skull, but I'll bet they could not have handled a rope for days after such treatment.

The only time one of them offered to get rough with me was when a loud-mouth in the seventeenth wagon decided I was too slow getting his mules to him the second morning I was there. He allowed as how he would haul me down off that horse and do some thumping on my ribs. This I was not willing to accept, especially as I was still tender in that region, so I showed him the front end of my Dragoon and he changed his mind.

The men in my mess were not so ornery and they were passing fair cooks, so we got along all right.

The heavy loaded train made about twenty miles a day, a bit more than you can take a herd of grazing cattle, so I was satisfied with the progress we were making. And like I said, the work was not overly hard. By the end of a couple weeks I was feeling almost as good as new, which was some kind of a relief. I am not cut out for the life of an invalid, I guess. It had rankled more than I would have expected when I had to be laid up for that period of time.

We reached Fort Dodge, the last army post offering protection on the trail for some hundreds of miles, and the men set up a grumble when Haven ordered the train past without giving the teamsters a chance to blow off their accumulated tensions.

Me, when I had delivered the mules to their proper wagons that next morning I ate and resaddled the chestnut. I found Haven finishing his breakfast.

"Mr. Haven, I need to talk with you a minute."

"Sure, Charlie." He brought a mug of coffee with him and walked with me away from the fire. "What is it?"

"Well, I figure I'm off duty now and on my own time. There's some business I need to attend to in Buffalo City. I will be back to the train before nightfall."

He gave me sort of a surprised look. "You didn't strike me as much of a drinking man, McMurty. I must say I didn't expect this."

"The fact is, I'm not much for liquor nor for beer either. Like I said, I have some business there. Or I might have. I don't think you want to know what it is." I looked him square in the eye when I said it.

"And if I don't give my permission?"

I shrugged. "Then I'll be saying good-bye. I've signed no articles of employment with you and would be violating no trust."

Haven fingered his chin for a moment. He said, "All right, but if there is any question about where you've gone I will say it is to hunt meat. If you see any game bring it back this evening. As a matter of fact, why don't you take Eric's horse along to pack in any meat you do shoot. Fresh meat would be welcome."

I grinned at him. "I was going to come back anyway if that is your way of having me carry along a sort of surety bond. But it suits me all right, and if I see anything worth shooting I will bring it back. Would you have a long gun I could borrow? All I have is my revolver."

"Sure." He motioned for Fortunada to join us. "Eric, McMurty here is going to scout for some fresh meat. I want you to let him use your horse and leave your Henry in the scabbard."

Fortunada looked puzzled. "This close to the fort? Don't you think the chances would be better tomorrow? Game should be pretty well shot out or spooked off this close in."

"I think now would be a good time, Eric." There was a layer of flint underlying Haven's voice, and Fortunada got the message all right.

"Whatever you say, John." He got his horse and led it to me, ramming a nearly new Henry rifle into a boot on the offside. "The rifle's loaded full," he told me when he gave me the reins, "and there's spare shells in my saddle pockets."

I thanked him and, since the rifle was on that saddle, mounted Fortunada's mare, leading my own gelding. I waved to them and turned the horses south.

Buffalo City was a growing collection of shacks and— mostly—tents about five miles west of Fort Dodge. The teamsters had been talking about it as a real mecca for those inclined toward the sinful pursuits, and I figured it would be almighty foolish for me to pass right by it without taking a look at it. It was not that I wanted anything the place had to offer, but I might find Lee Miles or Bud Terry there or at least word of them. It worried me to be so far behind them with no idea of where they might be.

I was not so much worried about finding them, really. I would do that. Soon or late, I would for sure do that. But they were bound to be spending money freely, and by now they could well have gone through all of it that had been mine and be starting on that which belonged to my neighbors. I really hoped to avoid that above all else.

When I saw it, Buffalo City turned out to be even less of a city than I expected. It was more a clutter of rags haphazardly suspended around collections of people, plank bars and whiskey kegs. I would not have thought there would have been enough freighters and buffalo hunters in the area to make it pay, but maybe the soldiers from the fort added enough to make business worthwhile. And maybe part of it was speculation with an eye toward the future. The railroad was building this way, and Buffalo City could become a shipping point then.

Anyway, it was not much of a place when I saw it. I had not come seeking to be impressed, though.

I tied the horses to the posts holding a poorly nailed and not strapped hitching rail. I didn't trust the rail itself.

I wandered around for a little while but saw no sign of either Lee or Terry nor of my sorrel or pretty, new saddle. I had not really expected to see them so was not disappointed that I did not. After a tour through the camp on foot I started at one end and began asking bartenders if they might have seen them.

Now those barkeepers were a rugged lot, most of them packing a heavy load of muscle and a collection of scars on their heads. I got the idea they were used to trouble and knew how to deal with it, as I guess anyone would have to be to do business in a place like this. The teamsters and the buffalo hunters too seemed to be on the prod when they were drinking, but both groups were more knives than guns.

I also found that those bartenders were not a talkative

lot. Under other circumstances I might have been more appreciative of men who left other people's business to those other people, but right now it was kind of vexing. I asked, and I asked but I got no word of the men I wanted to find.

Finally, in one crowded, rickety tent a fellow standing and watching a faro table overheard what I was asking. He turned and gave me a close look that I could not help noticing. I finished talking with the barkeeper and left, heading for the place next door.

I was out on the rutted street and about to turn in at the next tent when I happened to look back. That same fellow had come outside. He looked, spotted me and headed toward me.

The man was reasonably well dressed in a suit of brown linen, a fancy yellow vest that had some of its elegance taken away by being stained and spotted. He was wearing low-top shoes and was hat-less. As for the fellow himself he was tall, medium built and needed a haircut although he was clean shaven recently enough that he had no beard stubble to speak of.

"Were you wanting me?" I asked when he was a few paces away.

He slowed as he came near. He came to a stop and looked me over again before he answered. "You were asking after Bud Terry inside."

"I sure was. Would you know where I might find him?"

"Could be," the fellow said. He was fingering the pockets of his vest though he had no fob or watch chain there. "What do you want of him?"

"Now that's a real personal question, neighbor. I don't know as it concerns you," I told him, which may have been blunt but was a fact none the less.

The man shrugged. "Suit yourself. I just thought you wanted to find him."

"I told you I do. I just don't like to discuss other people's business with strangers."

"That sounds reasonable," the bareheaded man said, still fiddling with his vest pockets, "but I can't be pointing strangers at my friends either." He grinned. "Looks like an impasse, what?"

"Yeah. Well... the thing is, I'm not looking for Bud Terry so much as I am for a fellow with him. Lee Miles, it is. I have a message for Lee, and I hear he's riding partners with this Bud Terry." It was a lie of course, but I had a feeling I should be cautious with this fellow.

"You aren't a friend of Bud's?"

I shook my head. "Never met the man, but Lee and I come from the same county."

"What's your name?"

Well, I couldn't tell him what it was. I realized that right off. But I had not anticipated the question and did not know what to say. I blurted the first name I could think of—Jaimie Hunt—and hoped this fellow had not noticed a lag before I spoke.

"And you say you've never met Bud?"

"That's right."

I was about to breathe a little easier, but I should not have. The man gave me a sly look and said, "That's funny. I heard a fellow of that name rode with Bud and Miles a few months back. Could it be that you're lying to me?"

With no warning at all he had a derringer pistol in his right hand. It was pointed smack dab at my belly.

CHAPTER 8

"MISTER, YOU ARE MAKING YOURSELF A MISTAKE," I TOLD the man. He did not seem to be especially impressed.

That .41 caliber muzzle never wavered, and the man did not bat an eye. "Are you still trying to claim you're Hunt but you never met Bud?"

"No, I guess you have caught me out on that all right. But that gun of yours is starting to attract some attention. If you were to shoot it would give you a very bad name around here." I looked around us. It was true that people along the street were paying considerable attention to us. That pistol seemed to draw their attention like a magnet draws iron filings.

The man shrugged again. "No one around here cares, and even if they did there's not a one of them with guts enough to call me for it."

"I take it your name would be known then?" One corner of his lips curled back into a sneer. "Clay Tarrant," he said as if it were a threat, and I suppose it was.

I had heard of him before. He was said to be a

gambling man who was pure hell on wheels with a short gun and with a quick disposition to use one. A gambler and general no-good who had killed six or seven men across card tables.

"I still say you're making a mistake, Mr. Tarrant."

The sneer became more pronounced. "Now, why would that be?"

I forced myself to be calm and loose. I smiled at him, and while I don't know what he thought of that I know it helped me.

"Because if you don't tuck that little ole pistol back where it belongs, Mr. Tarrant, I will take the one shot you have there and put five others in your belly, sir." His eyes began to tighten, and I finished, "Bud Terry couldn't put me down with one shot, and I don't think you can either."

Now what I was thinking was that he would try to shift his aim toward my head, and that might give me a bit more time. Regardless, there was no point waiting around for it.

I didn't think about each movement I would have to make. I just sort of cut it loose and let all my practicing take over with what I had to do. I gave the signal to my arm and my old Dragoon was in my hand leaping from the recoil of the first shot.

I took a step backward and triggered another into Tarrant's body as his knees began to sag.

I expected to be feeling pain or some sort of shock of impact somewhere in my body and was surprised that I did not. I looked down at myself and only then realized that Tarrant had never gotten his shot off at me.

He was on the ground then, the derringer lying just in

front of him. He looked at it and then up at me. His eyes were glassy with shock, and he was nearly as pale as the collar of his shirt. His lips moved, and I knelt beside him, careful to pick up his pistol and slip it into my pocket so it would not be a temptation to him.

I bent close to the man. His eyebrows and lips stood out stark against his pale skin. Beads of sweat caught the sunlight on his forehead and along his upper lip.

"I think you've killed me, boy," he said in a hoarse voice. "I'll tell you the truth. I never saw anyone half so fast as you." His lips were getting redder. I thought for a moment his color was coming back but then I saw it was blood that was filling his mouth. He was dying, there was no doubt.

"I believe you're right, Mr. Tarrant. Is there anything I can do for you?"

He tried to grin. "No more than you've already done, boy." His eyes closed.

"Sir?"

The eyelids fluttered. "Yes?" His voice was a whisper now.

"I still need to know where I can find Bud Terry and Lee Miles. They took money that belonged to my neighbors, Mr. Tarrant. I have to get it back."

From somewhere he found the strength to laugh. "I swear I like you, boy. But pointing you toward Bud'd be like shooting him myself. A man doesn't... turn gun hawks loose on his friends, you know." He sighed and settled lower. I was not sure just when it was that he died.

I got to my feet. I felt a gut-wrenching sickness, sort of a numbness, deep inside me. I had never killed a man before. It was not a good feeling—one I could well have done without.

There were people all around me. I guess they had been there since Tarrant went down, but I had not been aware of them. One fat teamster was thumping me on the back. Others were grabbing at my hand trying to shake it. All of them were talking at once, jabbering congratulations and incredulity. They were telling each other—and me—what had happened.

At least I didn't have to worry about facing a murder charge. Most of the talk was about him already having a gun on me when I pulled. Well, to tell the truth I was some surprised myself that he hadn't got his shot off.

The crowd kept growing, the new arrivals getting the story from those who were there before them. Practically everyone was claiming to have seen it all with their own eyes though not more than a dozen or so had been nearby at the time.

Finally, an army officer shoved himself into the middle of things. As soon as he started acting bossy and asking official sounding questions, the crowd broke up and the men drifted off toward the saloon tents. I got the impression that I had really made the day for the whiskey peddlers closest to us.

The officer was a man with iron gray hair and a carriage and physique much like a cavalry saber. I wondered how anyone could tell when he was at attention and when he was at rest. He stood so straight in his Yankee uniform he seemed to vibrate.

"Captain Arthur Hall, sir, of Fort Dodge. You are the, uh, gentleman who had the altercation here?"

Well, I had no more use for blue-bellies than he seemed to have for Texans, and I was not about to back water for some Yankee with shiny brass buttons.

"It's none of your concern, mister," I told him. He didn't like that mister part. His expression did not change, but there was a tightening at the corners of his eyes.

"I could have you arrested."

"Now ah reckon you could try that, mister." I put my best, most Texan drawl in it. That Yankee did rankle me, and I was not in the mood for it just then. You have to say one thing for that rooster, though. The only thing he knew about me was that I'd just killed a man, but he was not backing down.

The captain was about to say something more but was stopped by a hand laid on his shoulder. A beefy, red-faced man with a brace of Colt's revolvers at his belt had come up beside him.

"I can handle it, Arthur. Thanks," the big fellow said. He had a rough and seedy look about him, but the feisty army captain nodded stiffly and walked away like he had a steel ramrod lashed tight to his spine.

The big man was not wearing a coat, but he did have on a fine vest of calfskin leather. It was old and cracked and plenty scarred but a fine article still. He dipped two fingers into one vest pocket and pulled out a silver colored metal disk. Deputy U.S. Marshal, it said.

"I'm Jim Peese," he said. "And you're?"

I gave him my name.

"Mind if I call you Charlie?"

I shook my head.

"Good." He laid an arm across my shoulders and turned me around. "Let me buy you a drink."

"Coffee'd be better."

"Fine," he said. He guided me in a new direction and pretty soon we were on stools in yet another tent.

"Now tell me what happened, Charlie," the deputy said after we'd been served.

So I did, telling it short and straight. The deputy was a man with the gift of being able to listen to someone. He gave the impression that I had every scrap of his attention the whole time I was talking, and I did not worry that he would get things twisted. When I was done he nodded.

"I'd say your story isn't as fanciful as most I heard already, but it seems to fit the facts all right," he said. "There won't be any trouble about it anyway."

"Can't say that I expected any, but I'm glad to hear you say it, deputy."

Again, he nodded. He asked, "You going to be around a few days?"

"No sir, I need to get back to work this evening, out on the trail with a mule train. Is there some reason I need to stay here?"

"There sure is. There's a paper out on Tarrant from New Mexico. It just came this morning, or you wouldn't have had your difficulty with the man."

"Is that where he came from before he arrived here?"

"Yes. He'd been here a few weeks, picking up a few dollars at the tables but causing no trouble until today. He mentioned Santa Fe several times, and that is where the flyer was issued. But say, aren't you even going to ask how much Tarrant is worth as cold beef?"

"Worth?"

"Sure. That's what I'm telling you. There is a price on his head. Five hundred, dead or alive. No questions asked. The flyer is issued by the marshal's office there, so I can pay you right here as soon as I confirm the identity of the dead man and get a coroner's jury together for the formalities." "Well, say now. I never shot that fellow for pay. I shot him because he had a gun on me and was fixing to shoot. That's the only reason, believe me."

"Oh, I believe you right enough." The deputy sipped at his coffee and stirred more canned milk into it. "Fact remains, you're clearly entitled to five hundred dollars cash money."

I shook my head. "Wow!"

The thing is, the idea of taking money for having killed a man was not the sort of thing I had ever envisioned as being a proper nor an honorable thing to do. Not that I had ever sat down and given thought to it before, but that was the way it struck me now that Peese raised the question. There was something about the idea that seemed wrong; immoral, I guess would be the best way to put it.

Yet at the same time, Peese said I was entitled to the money, that it was sanctioned by the law. And that was a chunk of money it would take an awful long time to earn at a wage of thirty dollars a month, which would be all I could expect if I took to punching cows or something like that. And that was all I really knew.

I guess by this point I was getting used to the idea, too, that Bud Terry and Lee Miles by now would have spent my share of the money they'd stolen and would be spending the part of it I still owed for the purchase of that herd. I would need to find some big chunks of money somewhere if I ever intended to pay off those debts. I pretty much had to take the money, and maybe it would not be a wrong thing to do if I did not take it for myself but to pay off the just debts I owed to my neighbors back home.

"Well, maybe you could give me a hand with it then, Mr. Peese," I asked of him.

"If I can, sure."

"You seem an honest man, marshal, the kind of man who takes his responsibilities serious and believes a deputy U.S. marshal's badge should mean something."

Peese threw his head back and roared with laughter, causing a good bit of head-turning among the other patrons of the dingy eatery. "Charlie boy, if you are spreading the butter onto me that thick, you must be about to ask a powerful favor. But I told you already. If I can do it, I will."

"Good. What it is, I need to get back to work right quick and won't be able to wait for you to get your jury to working. What I'd like is for you to send that money to my father back home. I could leave a letter for you to send along at the same time, so he'd know what I owe and where it should be paid. Would that be all right?" Mr. Shoup had explained to me how you could do that with just a piece of paper. If I'd known that before things might've been a lot different.

"Now I just reckon it would, Charlie. I'd be glad to do that for you."

"That takes something of a load off my mind, Mr. Peese. I appreciate it, I really do."

He nodded. "You said you were carrying money that belonged to your neighbors. Will this square you with them?"

Now it was my turn to laugh. "Lordy, Mr. Peese. I was owing thirty-eight thousand seven hundred and twenty dollars. Exactly. So, I guess I have aways to go before I'm square."

"And I thought I was being such a big help," Peese said with a shake of his head.

"You are, believe me," I told him. I finished my coffee. "It's people like you, marshal, that remind me there's decent folks around too. It is a good thing to remember."

"Yeah, well... I have paper and ink over at my office if you want to write that letter now." He drained off the last of his coffee and dropped a dime onto the counter. "Come on."

We ambled down the wide, rutted street, surrounded by noise and people and the pungent smells of a hard-drinking, male-dominated trading camp. The deputy seemed to be in his element here.

The office Peese took me to was another tent, but it did have a sturdy wooden frame and a plank floor, so I guess it was better than most of Buffalo City's business places at that. Peese waved me to one of two chairs in the place and took the other himself behind a huge desk. I hated to think what the freight costs on that desk must have been.

He found a clean piece of paper in one drawer and a steel tip pen in another. His ink bottle was dry, and he cussed some while he hunted for the powder to make a fresh bottle but after a while he had things assembled for me.

I wrote to Pa telling him only that I was all right and would he please put this money toward my debts and he could find the list in the top of the trunk at the foot of my bed. I told them not to worry and that I would be back when I could.

When I was done I got the envelope ready with the address on it and gave both to Peese for him to read if he wanted. He shook his head and folded the letter. He stuck it in the envelope without looking at it.

"That does it then, Charlie. I'll get it off in a few days. Soon as the coroner's jury can be seated, and that won't take long."

"Well, I sure do thank you, deputy." I stood and stuck out a hand, which he shook. I was real proud to shake with him, that was sure.

"Could I give you a word of advice, Charlie?"

"Of course."

"Maybe you won't need it. I hope you don't. But from what I've heard about the way you took Clay Tarrant today, you are almighty fast with that big Colt. I hope you won't let that go to your head. That kind of speed can make some men think they can do anything and get away with it. Like Tarrant. He felt that way, and now he's dead. I hope you won't go that same way. I really do."

He meant it too. That was plain to hear in his voice. But I didn't really understand what he was talking about.

"I hope so too, Mr. Peese. And thank you."

I left Peese at his desk and retrieved the horses I had

left down the street. You know something? Somewhere along in there I had quit worrying about killing Clay Tarrant. Maybe accepting the money had something to do with that. I don't know.

Whatever, I went back to the trail and turned west toward the train. I was even lucky enough to knock over a young, straggling buffalo bull before I reached them, and I had my horse draped heavy with fresh meat when I caught up to them. I think that surprised everyone in the train except maybe Haven. Not about the meat but about me coming back at all.

CHAPTER 9

"Why is everyone so nervous today?" I asked John Haven.

His beard quivered as he chuckled. "You'll see it soon enough if you're awake, but all the skinners know what we'll hit today. The Cimarron cut-off. Some call it the Journey of Death. A train can save nearly a month's travel on the cut-off. Or they can end up wiped out by lack of water or by hostile Indians. Comanches and Kiowas wander that country too frequent for safety. But using the cutoff makes a big difference in profits on a freighting venture, I can tell you."

"We'll be going that way then?"

"I did not say that, now did I?"

"You implied it well enough," I told him and used the last scrap of a biscuit to sop the remaining beads of congealing bacon grease from my pan.

"I did not," Haven said, grinning over the rim of his coffee mug. It was his habit to take his coffee with several different messes during each meal. Sometimes I wondered how the man was able to stay so heavy. He always seemed to be drinking coffee while the rest of us were eating.

"There's some—a good many—who use nothing but the cut-off," he explained, "but I'm not one of them. I like to make the best possible profit, but I try not to be a fool about it. So, my teamsters never know which way we'll be going until we reach the turning."

"Which way will we be going then?"

"Ah now, if I told you it would spoil the surprise for everyone, wouldn't it? But you should be able to figure it for yourself. Keep in mind that the deciding point is not Indians. There are times when a nanny could travel either route with a babe in a toddler's hand carriage and be perfectly safe, and there are times when you might have to fight your way through for weeks at a time which-ever way you go. No, the thing to worry about on the cut-off is water. That is where you can find problems that plain human cussedness can't overcome, you see."

Why, shoot, when he put it that way there was no trick to figuring what he would do. This late in the season it had been a good while since the rains, so if this was supposed to be a bad stretch ahead, most and maybe even all the surface water would be gone by now. And that would mean poor graze as well.

No, if I were doing it, say if I were taking a herd across, I would go the longer but better watered route and no doubt about it. Of course, John Haven was the boss of this train, not me, but he seemed to be a man who thought about the livestock he needed to move his goods as well as the value of those goods at the different ends of the

Santa Fe Trail. So, I was definitely betting that we would pass the southern cut-off and keep heading west today.

Haven drifted off toward another mess's fire, his coffee mug still in his hand. I dumped my eating gear into the big kettle and put my saddle and bridle in the big trailer behind the Deutsch wagon.

I climbed the ladder to the wagon box.

My blanket spread on top of those bolts of cotton yard goods sure looked good. I don't even remember hearing Deutsch and his son hitch their team.

When I woke up at dinner time everyone in the train was in a jolly humor. Kurt, old Fritz's boy, was whistling while he carried canvas buckets of water to the mules standing in their harness. The other teamsters, too, seemed to be feeling good. There was good, natural laughter and bantering insults passing from one wagon crew to the next. The Cimarron cut-off turning was behind us. I had missed seeing it, but that was all right. I wanted as little chance as possible of coming up against a band of hostile Indians. Or of peaceable, mule-robbing ones, for that matter.

The good feeling among the men continued for several more days as we followed the shallow, steady run of the Arkansas out of Kansas and into Colorado Territory. I believe it was nearly a week before any of the mule-skinners got into a brawl, so they must really have been happy with Haven's decision.

As we got further out from what passed for civilization in southwestern Kansas we began to see occasional scattered buffalo and so we almost always had fresh meat now. The thrifty train master had each animal skinned, and we packed the hides along for sale in Santa Fe or maybe back in Missouri at the end of the return trip.

I was disappointed there were no huge herds of the shaggy prairie cattle. As long as I could remember I'd heard tales of buffalo herds that could hold up travel for days while they streamed past on their migration paths, how you could look across their backs and see a regular ocean of brown bodies. These stories were told by men whose word I would trust, but all I saw for myself were widely separated animals moving singly or in small groups of no more than a dozen, and mostly fewer.

The other men with the train, some of them old hands who had been making the back and forth trip with Haven and for other businessmen for years, said they had often seen the great herds passing. They guessed that by now all the big herds were further south. Like I said, all I know about it is what I saw. But I do know the buffalo make awfully good eating, as good a piece of meat as anyone could ever want, and from a beef man that is saying something for sure.

I did not do any of the real meat hunting myself. Haven and Fortunada took care of that during the day while they were riding point and drag. Every once in a while, though, I would borrow a rifle and do some shooting. It was really something of a thrill after all I had heard about the huge, awkward looking beasts.

Let me tell you, though, there was nothing awkward about the way those shaggies moved. When you disturbed them or tried to run one from horseback, they could really scat. They could not stay ahead of a fresh horse going uphill but going downslope or on a level they were plenty fast on their feet.

I may as well admit that I succumbed to temptation once, as I guess any cowhand could understand. I just had to drop a rope on one of those devils.

It happened late in the afternoon when the train was already stopped for the night. We were still in Kansas, I believe. I had just wakened from a good sleep and was feeling pretty full of myself. I'd just finished saddling the chestnut and was fixing to go eat when a pair of grown cows and a half-grown calf legged it around to our side of a low knob. They weren't more than a few hundred yards away. And my rope was coiled at the side of my saddle, unused for weeks and weeks now. It was just too tempting to pass up.

I stepped onto the gelding and eased him away from the train. I took him at a trot away from the trio of buffs and around behind that knob, so they would not see me approach. I guess what I really had in mind was to do some showing off for those slow-moving teamsters as much as anything else.

As soon as the rise hid me from the buffalo I put the chestnut into a lope, so he would be nice and warm and set for a run. I circled around the knob and came up behind the cows and the bull calf. When they broke they did just what I'd wanted. They headed in a hard run down the length of the train.

I gave a whoop and thumped the chestnut in the ribs. That horse was not much for cutting but he knew what to do when his rider began to shake out a loop. He laid his ears back and dug his hooves in and got those long legs of his to churning. He could turn on some speed when he wanted and now, with those shaggies streaming out in front of him he wanted.

The calf was running in the rear of the procession and pretty quick the chestnut had him at his shoulder. The calf jinked to the left and back to the right, but the chestnut knew his business here and kept me in position for a throw. He darted with the calf just as pretty as you please, dipping his shoulders and powering ahead like the veteran he was. Off to the left I could hear the freighters shouting. They were yelling and waving their hats and generally carrying on in honor of the diversion. I believe they were urging the horse for more speed, not knowing he was in perfect position for my throw.

I've never been much for whirling a loop over my head and wearing my arm out for nothing. I gave it a quick spin to open the loop and let fly for the head. I suppose it would have been brighter to heel the little devil, so I could shake him loose when I was done playing with him, but I was thinking to get a solid catch around the neck and drag him back to the wagons for the amusement of the teamsters.

Well, I guess I never will know if you can make a pet out of a buffalo calf.

My loop slapped on true, and I threw my slack and sat back hard.

Now like every other ole boy from the south of Texas, I am a tie-fast roper and throw a short rope. I understand there are others who do it different, dallying a long rope with wraps around the horn, but tying fast to the horn is the way I learned and the way I've always done the job.

When the chestnut felt the shift of my weight he knew we were in business. He squatted on his haunches and shoved his front legs out straight, and that thousand pounds of horseflesh slid to a stop with his legs braced and the both of us ready.

Whoowee! but that little buff calf—he couldn't have weighed more than six, seven hundred pounds—made some rope pop and sing when he hit the end of it. He hit it hard and for his trouble got snatched clean around endwise and was spilled off his feet in a boil of dust.

No sooner had he gone down than he was up again and maybe because he was facing our way and had had his neck stretched more than was reasonable, he came a-charging.

He headed for the middle of the chestnut like he wanted to duck under the gelding's belly. The horse rolled its eyes and flicked its ears and made it plain he would prefer to leave the country. He was a stout-hearted beast, though, and went to running backward for all he was worth—doing his absolute damnedest to try and keep the slack out of that rope.

In the meantime, Mr. Calf veered enough to pass under the chestnut's nose, crossing from right to left at a full run.

There is no doubt that he had the steam up. He was tail up and moving hard when he hit the end of that rope the second time. Only this time the calf was crossways to us, and the chestnut was anything but braced for the shock; he was still churning backward trying to figure where the end of that rope had got to.

Well, he found out all right. The calf seemed this time

to have a better idea of what was coming when the rope came taut, and he flung himself into it for fair.

The horse went over sideways and me along with him. If I'd had any sense I would have jumped clear, but I did not. I guess I was just too interested in watching all this to think in terms of what I should be doing about it.

At a conservative estimate I would guess we put a bushel of dirt into the air.

The calf meanwhile was still driving and let me tell you those buffs have some power in their legs. He must have drug me and that horse—both of us squalling and kicking—ten yards or better before some generous providence snapped my rope.

The calf took off bawling after that pair of cows and soon was out of sight.

Me, I was left with torn britches, a tender-muscled horse and the ragged, frayed stub of what had been a darn good rope.

And I was not quite the hero I might have been among the teamsters, either. They had watched the whole thing, every lick and scratch of it.

CHAPTER 10

THE MULE DRAWN WAGONS CLOPPED ON ACROSS THE SHORT grass country along the Arkansas. The famous old trail pretty much followed the river so we were never overly far from water, which was downright necessary. That many mules can suck up a lot of the stuff, to say nothing of what us human type travelers needed. Twice each day I was especially glad Haven had decided to take the slower, safer route.

Not that Haven was giving up all that much, anyway. Some of the men in my mess were talking about it. They said our mule train would still make it in about the same amount of time as the bull teams drawn by oxen. I've seen a lot of ox carts down home. The Mexicans are high on those rigs for some reason. Any self-respecting land turtle moves faster. According to the boys in the mess, the advantage of the ox trains is that they are cheaper, taking fewer animals and less feed and you need only one bull-whacker per wagon instead of a muleskinner and his helper in trains like ours.

All of which, I guess, is beside the point. The point is that we kept moving along at a steady pace, and after a time we arrived at Bent's Fort— the stone one that they called the new fort although it looked plenty old to me. We passed it without stopping and went on that afternoon to an older place that was also called Bent's Fort. Whoever this fellow was, he must have had a powerful yen for the building of forts out in the middle of nowhere. I would guess he must have been in the business of trading with Indians or something, but when I was there the old fort was pretty much a refitting point for trains taking the trail down into New Mexico.

At least this Bent fellow had gone and built himself some proper forts when he did it. A lot of army posts are called Fort This or Fort That but all they really are is a bunch of regular buildings with maybe a packed earth square in the middle of them. Not Bent's Fort. This place looked like a fort, the sort of thing you imagine as a kid when someone talks about a fort.

The walls were tall and thick, built of adobe so no one could ever shoot through them or burn them or otherwise hurt them in any way that I could ever think of. Grander yet, two opposing corners of the fort had round towers sticking out from the walls and built even higher. The tops of the walls and the towers had firing ports cut into them, so the gate and every scrap of wall could be covered by riflemen. For some reason it gave me quite a thrill to see that big old fort out here so far from civilization.

Of course, there were no longer any troops there, if there ever had been. When I saw it the big gate on the north wall—the only gate, for that matter—had pretty much fallen apart and was just so much cracked and weather-silvered wood.

Inside there were adobe walled rooms all the way around the walls, the ones to the right and straight ahead being two-story affairs and the rest with their roofs serving as a ramp so people might have once stood at the firing ports. Now the rooms were taken up by several businesses such as a blacksmith and a wheelwright and a harness maker and by a few small-time traders who had ragged piles of furs thrown in the corners and who offered such junk as a heathen might admire. There were also a couple prosperous looking men offering liquor and some greasy looking Indian women. It was to them that the muleskinners headed, first thing.

Me, I had it pretty easy. Attached to the back of the fort there was an adobe walled corral where we put the mules as soon as they were unhitched, so I didn't have a thing to do while we were stopped there.

We hazed the mules inside and pulled some poles across the corral gate opening and that was that. I was a bit surprised when John Haven walked over to me and laid a hand on my shoulder.

"Come on, Charlie. I'll buy you a drink."

"Sure," I said. We went around the walls to the entrance and inside where the men were already gathered and laughing.

You wouldn't think that forty-six muleskinners could make so much noise or get themselves drunk so fast, but the fort was a regular madhouse of shouting and laughing and clog dancing already. Even the Deutsches were there, perched on a pair of hogsheads with tin mugs in their hands, singing songs to each other in German.

Eric Fortunada was off to the left under one of the towers having a long talk with the blacksmith, who was looking pretty satisfied with the world. He would be getting a lot of business the next day resetting tire rims and replacing chain and S-hooks and such.

Haven waved me down on a bale of pelts dumped on the ground by a doorway, so I sat there and waited while he went inside. When he came back I was glad to see he was carrying mugs of beer, which if I am going to take a drink of something I prefer over whiskey.

I tasted of it and it was pretty good, which I told him.

"You bet," he said. "Lemp's. I hauled twenty-four hundred gallons of it out here the last trip I made. I would've taken it on to Santa Fe, but Murdoch offered such a good price for it I couldn't refuse. I'll carry more next spring, I think."

"You haul for yourself then, not on contract?"

"Sure do. More risk, but there's more money in it too. A man could do a lot worse."

"Yes sir." Well, what else should I say? He seemed a nice enough fellow and had a right to be proud of being good at what he did.

"I've been watching you, Charlie. You don't shirk, and you know livestock. Knowing your animals and keeping them fit is a big part of freighting if you're to do well with it."

"Yes?" The man had something in mind.

"I won't lie to you, Charlie. The days of the trail are numbered now. The railroads are building this way fast, and there won't be any way to compete with them once they make it through. But for the next few years a man can still turn a handsome profit, and later... well, I know the market. I know what to buy and when to sell, and I'll be pretty well fixed for brokering goods even after the rails build through. Until then I want to make all I can on these mules and wagons."

"Sounds reasonable," I said, just to be saying something.

"What I want to do is put a second train to work, double my trade while I can, you see. Now Eric has been with me three years. He knows skinners and he knows wagons. The only thing he doesn't know is mules and grass and water. That part of it, you know. I could put you and Eric together on one train and take the other myself. Cut both of you in for a part of the profits, you see? It could be a good thing for you. I dare say you could earn a thousand dollars a year or even more. What do you think?"

Now that did not take much thinking about, though it was awfully nice of him to make the offer. "Well, I thank you, Mr. Haven, but I'm a cowman at heart. This business of commerce and trade and such just isn't for me. And ... anyway ... I have a powerful debt to be paid off and don't know but one way I'll ever be able to do it. So, I thank you, but I'll have to refuse."

Instead of looking disappointed Haven's eyes sort of lit up. "You needn't be so quick to say no, Charlie. If you're in debt maybe we can work that out between us. You could, say, sign a note to me payable with your services.

Something like that, you see. That could work out very nicely."

Now I guess it could. Mr. Haven was thinking he could have a hired hand who'd be locked to him hard and fast with the backing of any state or territorial court in the land. I'll just bet that is exactly what he was thinking.

"Well sir, I just might have to consider something like that, Mr. Haven. I swear I'd have to. You say you'd pay off my debts, and all I do is sign a note and work for you to pay it off until I'm clear again?"

"That's right, Charlie. That's all there would be to it. My attorney in Santa Fe could draw it up properly to protect us both, you see?" He sort of laughed. "One thing I've learned over the years is that cowmen are generally men of their word, Charlie. Take their debts seriously even if they do tend to use a gun instead of a legal paper. So how much do you want that note for? Just give me the figure, and we'll shake on it."

"Yes sir," I said. I grinned at him and stuck my hand out. "Just a bit over thirty-eight thousand dollars and you have yourself a boy, Mr. Haven." He was reaching for my hand sort of automatical like, with a big smile on his face, when the words sunk in. He blanched, and his hand stopped in mid-air.

"Did you say thirty-eight thousand dollars?"

"Yes sir, I sure did." I shook my head. "I reckon the cow business can be a bit chancy too, but it's powerful good when you make it."

"Surely you don't ... I mean you couldn't expect, on just a handshake..."

"Why, that's how I got it to start with, Mr. Haven, was on a handshake. There's not a man down home who's carrying a signed note from me. And there's not a one will have to go unpaid, either. Like you said, I take such things serious."

Haven gave a quick, vigorous shake of his head and got to his feet. "Look here now, McMurty, you were misleading me there. I don't like that."

I got a cold feeling inside me. Up until now I'd been just playing. I guess maybe Haven saw something in my face that showed what I was thinking just then. He took a step backward and looked like he'd been punched in the stomach. "That isn't what I meant, McMurty. No offense. Really."

He turned and walked quickly away, and I sat and wondered what he could have seen in me to scare him so. For he was scared, and I had never thought of myself as being the kind of person to bring that sort of response from another grown man. It was strange, but I had no answers to it and after a while quit wondering and went off to climb into one of the old towers, so I could get a better look at Pike's Peak showing plain to the west.

After that day, though, John Haven kept his distance from me and from that time on never again called me Charlie. It was always just McMurty the few times he did speak. Which was all right by me and did not stop me from giving him a full day's work for the food and the pay he'd be providing me with.

We laid over two days at Bent's fort while the blacksmith shrank, and refitted tire rims and the wheelwright tightened spokes on those huge, deeply dished wheels and others worked at their craft to make sure the tongues and the trees and axles and straps were in good shape. Most of the muleskinners got themselves so well loosened during those two days and three nights that I believe they were glad to be back on the road when we finally turned south away from Arkansas, crossing and leaving it a half dozen miles beyond the fort.

Away from the river were dry sand hills with nothing much to recommend them and later yet were steeper, rocky hills which led smack into the mountains and Raton Pass.

I guess if I'd been cut out to be a freighter I would not have so much liked that passage through the mountains, for the road was poor, rocky and often steep, and I suppose it must have played hob with the heavily loaded wagons. It was sure they moved slowly and with the benefit of heavy cussing during that part of it.

From my viewpoint, though, I got quite a charge out of it. Being from flat country myself I had never seen anything nearly so spectacular as the peaks around Raton Pass, and I spent a good bit of my sleeping time on the wagon box beside Kurt Deutsch, so I could see what all we were passing over, around or beneath.

It is such a country as to make a man want to breathe extra deep for the pure joy of it and I began wondering how cattle would do in high country, and sure enough in the meadows above a village called Mora there were some beeves pastured. I was really sorry when the train left the pass behind and dropped down to open country again.

Pretty soon we were back into settled country with ranches and small towns, though with a higher number of Mexicans here than can still be found around home. I guess that can be understood, though. People hereabouts would not have quite the same feeling toward Mexicans since they would not likely have lost kin at the likes of Goliad, which still rankles in the minds of most whose people have been any length of time in the Lone Star. Still, it was kind of surprising to find Mexicans who acted like they were as good as anybody else, and I did some thinking on that and decided my best bet on that subject would be to keep my mouth shut and my eyes open, which is what I did.

We pulled into Santa Fe about three weeks after leaving the Arkansas, and I found that I was pretty well pleased with it. You could see white-topped mountains hanging over the town, and everyone around seemed friendly enough.

The wagons were lined up for unloading in the yard attached to a long, low adobe walled building and the mules were unhitched and turned over to a crew of Mexican hostlers and my job was done from that point on, so I rolled my bedding and saddled the chestnut and went to find John Haven.

Haven was in the office part of the long warehouse talking with a man who seemed to be his local agent, and the both of them smiling and in good humor so I judged it a fine time to draw my pay and shake hands and be shut of the man.

When he saw me Haven forgot to scowl. He even said, "Did you hear that, McMurty? Bill Anders started out not more than a week behind me. Took the cut-off to save time. Ha. He lost two men and a wagon, had seven mules killed and just beat me by three days for his pains. Didn't save a thing when you consider those losses. I guess I know what I'm about with this business." The other fellow was smiling and agreeing with him.

"Well, I guess you do, Mr. Haven, and I've enjoyed seeing the way a train is run. I really have. But I have to get on about my own business now."

"Fine, McMurty. You do that now. You just do that. And say, you did all right with those mules. You can ride along with me any time, and it is always safer in a strong party than alone. I was glad to have your company."

He was in a fine, expansive mood, he was, but here on his safe and civilized home territory it was easy to see where he was going. Well, I was not backing down.

"You seem to be forgetting the forty dollars you owe me, Mr. Haven."

He stepped closer and laid a meaty hand on my shoulder and smiled at me through his beard. "Now if you recall, that was a tentative agreement, McMurty, and certain other things did not work out. Why, back at Buffalo City I believe you even reminded me that you were not subject to formal articles of employment. So, I am sure you will agree that our original thoughts did not work out." He gave my shoulder a squeeze. "But don't you worry about a thing, McMurty. We did enjoy your company, and you were welcome to all our food. No charge for that. None at all."

I felt the heat rising within me. I shook his hand from my shoulder and stepped back a pace, conscious of the big Dragoon at my belt. "I don't think we are going to do it that way, Haven. You offered employment, and you got every hour of work you asked for. Now you'll pay me the forty dollars, and I'll thank you to pay it now. In coin if you please. I don't believe I would want your paper."

Haven was still smiling. "You needn't take on so, McMurty. We seem to have an honest difference of opinion here. If you feel all that strongly about it you can always seek relief before a territorial court, my boy. But, uh, you have no signed articles to present. I doubt you would succeed. But file if you wish. You have that right, you know. And either way I harbor no harsh feelings, my boy. No indeed, nor do I intend to, either."

The man thought he had me stuck, here where he was known and more than likely was a friend of each and every judge in this territorial seat.

"Haven, you said yourself that cowmen are notional people. Well, I guess that is the truth. So, the way it is, I will not be filing any court papers. You aren't worth the bother, Mr. Haven. Either you pay me what you owe me. ..." I paused deliberately and looked him square in the eye, or you don't..."

The assurance drained out of his face. "And if I don't?"

"Then I'll shoot you here and now in front of that witness who would have to testify to your fraud. And I'll take my forty dollars off your body."

"Now listen here, McMurty, this is Santa Fe. You can't get away with such behavior here," he blustered.

I shrugged. "You'll never know if I get away with it or not, John Haven."

His friend interrupted. In a soft voice he warned, "John, I wouldn't push if I was you. Anders was saying that a young fellow named McMurty killed Clay Tarrant at Buffalo City. They say Tarrant had his gun drawn and leveled before the other fellow bothered to go for his." At least it was interesting to know how the story had been distorted away.

Haven glared at me with suspicion, but I do not believe the man was ready to back down. The cloak of Missouri law and order must have seemed too strong here where he conducted his business. Well, I didn't figure to take water from him, either. I'd told him what I would do. And I would do it.

The agent, or whoever the other man was, stepped between us and dug a hand into his pants pocket. He looked back and forth from Haven to me. "No need for trouble now, so the both of you calm down. McMurty? You said you are owed forty dollars? Here," he pulled some change from his pocket and picked out four eagles. He extended them to me.

A retort rose to my lips. I was set to demand that John Haven pay what he owed me himself. If he did not I was set to put a soft lead ball through his breast bone. I was set to pull the Dragoon when I remembered what Deputy Peese had told me, and of a sudden I was ashamed of myself. I would have taken the man's life simply because he was a petty cheat. Instead I nodded and put out a hand to accept my pay.

I do not think John Haven knew how close he had come to being shot. But the experience kind of shook me. I took my money and left.

CHAPTER 11

THE SALOON OF THE BIG HOTEL ON THE SQUARE WAS FULL but it wasn't rowdy. The noise was more like a steady buzz, and no one was making a nuisance of himself, which I liked.

They served food as well as drinks there. I found myself a table in a corner and ordered a tallow-fried steak and a mess of boiled eggs, which is one of the nicer things about being back in settled country. I really like an egg and had been missing them while traveling.

Another of those nicer things was seeing a pretty girl again. And, boy, was there a pretty one there!

I'd never seen a girl waiting tables in a public restaurant and saloon before, but here no one seemed to think a thing about it. This girl was Mexican but with a light, smooth, soft complexion and likely no Indian blood in her as so many have. And was she pretty? I'll tell the world she was. Dark hair and big, dark eyes. Thin but built more delicate and lithe than puny. She definitely did not look puny. If it hadn't been for thoughts of Evelyn Stewart back home I think I would have been tempted to linger and see could I talk with her some.

As it was this girl brightened my meal by being the one to bring it, and I enjoyed the food all the more because of the service.

I was just finishing a last cup of stout coffee when a man I did not know slipped into the chair opposite me at my table. I thought that odd but perhaps another of the different customs here until he asked if I was Charles McMurty.

"I am," I admitted, "but if we've ever met I am afraid I've forgotten it."

"No, we haven't," he said. Without explaining further right away he caught the eye of the little serving girl. She rushed over with a bright smile putting extra light into her eyes. "Mr. McMurty and I need a pot of coffee here, Juana, and I'll need a cup." She bobbed her head prettily and darted away with a flare of her skirts.

"That's real generous of you I'm sure, but I'd still sorta like to know who you are."

"Of course. Jason Kalb, duly elected county sheriff. And you, I believe, are the gunfighter I've heard so much about these past few days."

"Gunfighter?" Now that took me by some surprise. Just about the last thing I wanted in this world was to get a reputation like Clay Tarrant or J.W. Hardin or one of that stamp of law-breaking fool.

"Mr. Kalb, someone has been giving you some wrong information, sir. My ambitions are strictly in the line of good cows and heavy calf crops. And a certain little gal back home. No sir, I am no gunfighter by any means. No sir."

"Now I am real glad to hear that, Mr. McMurty. Perhaps someone told me wrong when they said you killed Clay Tarrant a few months back."

"Well," I said, a bit uncomfortably, especially as I had come so close to a second shooting not an hour earlier, "I guess I would have to admit that I shot the man. But he honestly did force me to it. There were plenty of witnesses to what happened. And I'm sure no gunfighter. I never busted a cap at another man, before nor since, and if I'm lucky I won't ever have to again. Really."

Kalb shook his head. "I wouldn't count on being so lucky, McMurty. Tell me about it."

So, I did, making as much of a point of the self-defense angle as I could without stretching the facts. The girl brought our coffee in the middle of the telling, and Kalb sipped at it while he listened. Well, it was not a real long story. The cup she had poured for me was still warm when I was finished talking.

The sheriff grunted and said, "You say Tarrant was fixing to shoot. How were you sure?" "Well, he surely acted like he was going to shoot. And he had a pistol in his hand. I surely did figure he was going to use it."

"That part is true then? He already had his gun out?"

"Yes sir, he did."

"I will confess that that part of it surprises me, McMurty. I swear it does, even though men in the Anders train brought exactly that story with them from Kansas. But I thought, well, that it was just another of those exaggerations that abound in gunfight stories. You must be awfully fast, McMurty. I saw Clay Tarrant kill a man here some months ago, and I thought then that he must have been the fastest draw alive. If you're faster, you must be pure hell with that six-gun. Sure, hope you don't get too free with it."

"I don't plan on it, Mr. Kalb. Like I told you, I am no gunfighter. I don't want to be one. And I don't intend to be one."

"I'm real happy to hear that, McMurty. Surely am. I wouldn't want the two of us to have any trouble." He drained his cup. "So, if there is ever any way I can help to, uh, avoid trouble in my county, you just let me know, hear?" He started to rise.

"Mr. Kalb?"

"Yes?" He sat back down.

"Why don't you pour yourself another cup there, sheriff. Since you brought it up, sir, you just might be able to help with what brought me here." He poured himself the coffee before he nodded. "All right. Try me."

I told him about Lee and Bud and why I was looking for them, and again he listened patiently until I was done talking.

"Hell, McMurty, you're asking me to finger those men for a shoot-out. What I offered to do was avoid trouble, not bring it on quicker and surer than you might do on your own."

"No sir, Mr. Kalb. That isn't what I had in mind at all. Not at all. You see, what I want is to get back the money those fellows took. At least the amount that belongs to my neighbors, the ones I got my herd from on tick. I owe that money. I figure to pay it. That's all."

"You don't figure to go to shooting the first thing then?"

"Good heavens no, Mr. Kalb. Why, those boys might have put my money in a bank or something. If I up and shot them first thing then I'd never be able to get my neighbors' money back for them. What I want to do is shake them up, not shoot them down. And, anyway... Lee Miles and I grew up together. I wouldn't want to have to face his daddy someday and tell him I'd shot Lee. I wouldn't want that."

"No, I reckon you might not at that."

"So, I really do hope you will help me."

"Have another cup while I think on this, McMurty."

He poured for me—it was still fairly hot—and I sipped at it while Kalb concentrated on his own cup of the stuff.

I began to realize that if I stayed away from home and from the cattle trails very much longer I would pretty soon start taking my coffee plain as a matter of course. The Missourians along the trail and now these people in Santa Fe seemed to serve it that way as if it was the normal and natural thing to do. Already I had got used to taking it that way, though I could not say it was my preference. I still would've liked having my canned cow and some short sweetening to drop in there.

"They were both here," Kalb said at length. "They showed up, oh, two and a half, maybe three months ago. Bud Terry I've known for some time. He shows up every so often. Likes to live it up when he does. Good liquor. Pretty women, and lots of them. He likes to buck the tables, too. High stakes when he can. A lot of brass and bluster all the time."

"He must have really been down on his luck to take a common ol' job with the likes of us," I offered.

"Maybe. Or maybe he had you in mind all along as a fat score."

"Aw, but if that was so, what would he want with Lee?"

Kalb grimaced and held his palms upward. "I wouldn't know. Could be he thought having a friend of yours along would make things go easier. Or maybe Miles got wind of what Terry intended so he cut Miles into it, so he wouldn't tip you beforehand. You may never know the answer to that."

"I guess it isn't important except for my own curiosity anyway. What I need to know for sure, though, is where I can find those boys. That I do need, Mr. Kalb."

"Yes." He looked uncomfortable. "Terry left. At least a month ago. Your friend Miles is still around." He stopped, and after long moments I quit waiting and prodded him.

"Well?"

"You won't like it."

"I wasn't crazy about the idea of them robbing me to start with, sheriff. I didn't really expect to enjoy the rest of it."

"All right. Come on then." He got to his feet and rang a silver cartwheel onto the table. "My treat," he said.

Kalb led me through the maze of people and tables to a side door that opened onto one of the narrow streets that twisted away from the sun-dried square. I was glad I had a guide who knew where he was going for I'd have been lost halfway there even though it was only a couple minutes away. The place was in an alley that I would've taken for just a space between buildings.

Kalb came to a heavy, crudely built door that he pushed open without knocking. Darned if the place wasn't a cantina of sorts. The customers were a collection of the meanest looking Mexicans I had ever laid eyes on. These were not the quiet, hard-working people we had back home nor the open faced, easy going Mexes I had seen so far in New Mexico Territory. These here were hardcases who made it easier for me to understand Santa Ana's butchery those years back before I was born.

Once inside the sheriff didn't even have to look around. He knew just which corner to go to. He plucked a lantern from the wall as he went and held it high, so I could see.

In the feeble, yellow light I could see a pile of rags on the floor. I looked closer and saw a grimy, bewhiskered American there. The man blinked and snorted. "My God!" he cried. He tried to crawl backward but was blocked by the dirty adobe at his back. He hid his face in the corner.

It was hard for me to accept that this was Lee Miles. But it was so.

CHAPTER 12

KALB HELPED ME LIFT LEE, SUPPORTING HIM BETWEEN US with his head nodding and bouncing freely. It was a generous thing for Kalb to do, really. At such close-range Lee smelled pretty awful.

"You'll have to take him out of here if you want to talk to him," the sheriff said. "You wouldn't get far with him here. They must have some sort of money stake in him, the way they keep him full of cheap tequila all the time. Been doing it for weeks now."

I nodded. Didn't want to open my mouth to speak. It would not have seemed clean somehow. Lee was draped half onto my shoulder, practically, and I had my left arm wrapped around his waist. The sick, sour odors coming off him and out of his clothes were thick enough I thought I might taste them if I opened my mouth to speak.

We dragged him out of the dark corner toward the doorway. His feet scraped along the packed clay floor. He was not even trying to support any of his own weight.

The Mexicans in the cantina glared at us but did not speak. The whole place was dead quiet except for our grunting and the scrape of Lee's boots being drug.

We were near the door—and the fresher air of the alley—when someone outside shoved it open and stepped in. He was a short, slim built little Mexican duded up in fancy clothes with a wide sash and a small, nicely creased felt hat. He took on a big smile when he saw Kalb, and I thought at the time he was the first one I'd seen in this cantina that didn't look like some kind of cut throat bandito or general no-good.

The sheriff seemed surprised to see him there, judging from the look on Kalb's face. He stopped moving and of course I had to wait too.

"Gaspe! I'll be damned," Kalb said. The Mexican grinned at him all the bigger.

"I have papers on you, Gaspe. You're under arrest," Kalb said.

Which was a brave thing for the man to say, I will tell you. Mr. Kalb had his right hand full of Lee Miles and his left still occupied with the lantern he'd taken off the wall. And here he was, putting someone under arrest.

Gaspe never said a word but of a sudden there was a flicker of light on shining metal, and he took a slash at Kalb's neck. The sheriff tried to twist out of the way but there was a spray of red in the air.

Me, I never had time to think what to do, but I guess those Kansas jackrabbits had taught my hand more than my brain. The Dragoon was in my fist and rolling before I had time to decide about it, and Gaspe went staggering back with a ball in his chest. The knife fell gleaming in the open doorway, but it was less shiny now.

The Mexican fell down in the trash of the alleyway and curled himself into a tight ball.

"At least that smoke smells better than your friend."

Kalb was sitting on the floor by the leg of a table. He had his gun in one hand. With the other he was using a handkerchief to stop the blood from a long cut on his cheek.

Lee was still supported against my left side. I had forgotten him there for a little while. Now that I remembered him I could no longer hold him by myself and he slid down until he was on the floor too, slumped against my leg.

"Damnation," Kalb said in a mild tone of voice. He brushed broken glass aside from where the lantern had fallen and got carefully to his feet. "You just cost me some money, boy. But I guess I'll thank you anyway. He was mighty swift with that knife."

Kalb walked outside, gun in hand, and nudged Gaspe with his toe. He needn't have bothered being so cautious. The little man was dead. Kalb shoved his revolver back into his holster and retrieved the knife from the doorway. It was a wicked looking thing, the stains on the blade already turning brown as they dried. Kalb looked at it and shook his head and tucked the knife behind his gun belt. "Nasty things, knives. I don't like 'em.

I was still rooted in the same spot with Lee flopped up against me. I still had the Dragoon in my hand. It was cocked and ready to go again. I let the hammer down to half cock and turned the cylinder so there would not be a live cap under the striking face. I put it away.

The sheriff watched me. When I was done he said, "No wonder Tarrant got his surprise. I didn't know anybody could be that quick. Not that I'm complaining, mind you!"

"Yeah, well ... I wouldn't know about any of that. I'm just sorry it happened."

And I guess I was in a way, but really that was more the words I expected of myself than it was what I was thinking and feeling. Because for some reason I was feeling less about shooting Gaspe than I had when I shot Clay Tarrant. Yet Tarrant had been trying to kill me. The little Mexican had been no threat to me at all. For all I knew Mr. Kalb could and would have protected himself just fine since that first sweeping slash did not do serious damage. I realized this at the time and tucked it away in the back of my head to be brought out and chewed over when I had the time. For now, there was Lee to be thinking of.

"He has relatives in town," Kalb said with a look at Gaspe. "I'll send someone to tell them. They'll want to see him buried properly, I know." He went behind the bar and spoke briefly with the man there. When he came back he bent again to help me with Lee. The cut on his cheek had quit bleeding.

For the second time we hauled Lee Miles' limp body upright between us. By the time we were out of the alley to an almost normal street—none of them seemed to be very wide around this town—I could feel the beginnings of resistance in Lee's own legs. He was a long way from walking, but it seemed there was hope he would come out of it eventually.

Kalb flagged down a fellow in a spring wagon to carry us back toward the big square.

"Where do you want him?"

"I don't hardly know," I told him. "I haven't got around to looking for a room yet. Could you recommend something on the cheap side?"

"You bet I could." He crab-walked forward across the bed of the moving wagon and gave the driver instructions to go to a street the name of which I do not remember, to a boarding house run by a man named Fetchler.

I was pretty thoroughly lost by the time we got there. It is a good thing I did not have to navigate on my own. I can take off cross country and come out right on the button at any pass, peak or valley once the lay of the land has been described to me, but those Santa Fe streets were plain too much for me. No contest to it..

Kalb thanked the driver of the spring wagon and we dragged Lee—stiff-legged now—up a short run of steps to a broad, covered porch tacked onto the front of an otherwise perfectly normal adobe house. The sheriff helped me ease Lee into a rocking chair on the porch and said, "Be right back," then disappeared inside without knocking.

In a few minutes he was back, along with a middle-aged fellow with thinning hair and a pot belly that stuck out between the uprights of his galluses. Kalb introduced him as Byerly Fetchler.

"Lead the way, Bye," he said.

We muscled Lee out of the chair and hauled him

inside to a rear room. Fetchler looked like he was willing to stay and chat a while, but the sheriff gave him a pointed sort of look. "Dinner at six in the front room," he said on his way out the door.

There was not much in the room. A bed with a thin coverlet; a stand with a crockery bowl and water pitcher, empty. Another stand, bare. No chairs or even a wardrobe. Luxury it was not, but it was clean.

Lee was not clean. I held him up while Kalb stripped the stinking clothes from him. The sheriff took the clothing and pitcher and left the room. He came back with only a full pitcher of water.

"Fetchler has a Mexican lady who does the cooking and cleaning. She was clucking and carrying on, but she said she'll wash that stuff and patch it up. She'll leave it outside your door before she goes home this evening whether the stuff dries or not."

"Fine. Is there a rag in that pitcher?"

"Yeah. And I got some soap."

I had laid Lee on the floor rather than taking a chance of fouling my bed. I did not know how often they changed their bedding here, and I sure would not want to live with that smell for any length of time. Kalb helped me wash the drunkenness off the outside of Lee. There were no towels handy but if Miles did not like the treatment maybe he shouldn't have made it necessary. It sure was more pleasant in the room when we were done. Lee, though, was still pretty well out of touch with the world. I doubt he felt any of it.

Kalb stood wearily and looked at Lee lying there on the floor, wet and snoring loudly. Kalb shook his head.

"Sheesh! He's about as bad as they come. No point in me waiting around for him to wake up; that could take a couple days."

"Yes sir. I sure appreciate all your help, though."

"You appreciate my help? Come on now! Gaspe might have split me open like a fresh caught fish. I'd say that I owe you, McMurty." He sighed and rubbed the back of his neck. "Look, your horse is still over at La Fonda. I need to stop in at the office, but I'll put your animal in at Jorge Sanchez's livery. This evening I'll bring your bedroll and saddle bags around and see if Mister Lily of the Valley there decided to come back to life, okay?"

"You bet, Mr. Kalb."

He took off, and I flopped on the bed for lack of anything better to do. There was nothing to read, nothing to see or listen to except for Lee and his snoring. And I did not want to set myself yet to thinking about Gaspe. So, I stretched out and napped a while.

Kalb did not return until after supper—which was pretty good and there was lots of it—and when he did he was carrying my things as he had said he would do. Lee was still out, but now he seemed to be more asleep than passed out. At least he was not snoring quite so heavily.

"Might be able to wake him now," I offered. "I take it you'd like to listen when I talk to him?"

"I'd rather."

I knelt beside the man who used to be my friend and shook him around some. He stirred and after enough of it groaned and opened his eyes, at least by a narrow slit. He was squinting and blinking considerable, but he did seem to know there were people around. He took to mumbling.

"Why don't you get some coffee and maybe a dry biscuit for him?" Kalb suggested. "It's hard to say how long it might have been since he ate anything."

I did as he asked. The Mexican lady who did the work around the place was in the kitchen putting the last touches on Lee's clothes, so I carried them back too.

When I returned, Kalb had Lee seated on the side of my bed. He was able to hold himself upright. It is for sure he could see and recognize people.

When I stepped in through that door Lee saw me. His eyes went wide, and his jaw dropped open and he let out a bleat like a doggone sheep caught between fence poles. He looked scared half to death. I had forgotten that Lee would still believe me dead from Bud Terry's bullet.

Lee closed his eyes tight. When he opened them again, though, I was still there.

"Do you figure you've gone to hell, Miles?" Kalb asked.

He looked at the sheriff. Kalb said, "You remember me, Miles. You've spent a night or two in my cell, remember?" Lee nodded.

"Right," Kalb said. "Now turn around and greet your old friend. He's come a long way to find you." He took Lee none to gently by the jaw and forced his head around my way. Lee's mouth tried to work but he was not making any noises.

"What's the matter, Lee?" I asked. "No questions about the folks back home? Not going to ask about my health? Well, ol' buddy, I have a few questions for you."

Lee closed his eyes.

"You can't make me go away that easy, Lee. You're just going to have to face me."

"You might as well, Miles," the sheriff put in. "I can hold you for extradition on this man's testimony, you know. Armed robbery and attempted murder at the least. You could be looking at twenty years. Maybe as much as forty."

Lee opened his eyes. "It is you, Charlie?" he whispered.

"You just bet it is, Lee ol' buddy. I came looking for some money you boys took."

Kalb snapped his fingers like he'd just remembered something, but he did not say anything just then.

"I thought Bud'd killed you. I sure did," Lee said. He was still having trouble believing what he saw.

"Where is the money, Lee?"

He tried to feel of his pants pockets and only then discovered he was naked. He seemed to cringe even more then, if that was possible. His mouth worked and after a few false starts he said, "Bud. He has it, I reckon. I don't know."

"What've you been drinking on all this time, Miles?" Kalb asked. "How have you paid for all that tequila?"

Lee's brow furrowed. "I think . . . Bud . . . paid them . . . said he would pay them. Something like that. I don't remember. Not for sure."

"Is Bud coming back here?"

Lee shrugged.

"Where did he go?"

"Somewhere. Left me. Took my share too. Him and... Childress? Yeah. Little Jimmy Childress." I looked at Kalb and raised an eyebrow. The sheriff nodded. "Little Jimmy Childress. Heads a bunch of wild ones. If Terry put in with them he must like this robbery business, for that is what they do best. They were through here a while back, but they didn't stay long." There was satisfaction in the sheriff's voice when he said that last part.

"Where'd they go, Lee?"

"I don't know. Arizona. Maybe California."

Again, I looked at the sheriff. "There is some mining activity in Arizona," he said, "and the territory is poorly organized. It could be. Wherever they are, they'll be on the owl hoot trail, you can count on that."

"Get dressed, Lee."

He looked scared. "I don't have a gun."

"Just get dressed." He did. When he was done I told him, "Go find yourself a place to sleep tonight. Be back here first thing in the morning. And if you take so much as one drink, I'm going to shoot you down like a hydrophoy skunk. I'll decide tomorrow what to do about you."

There was a look of relief on his pale features. Lee bobbed his head and practically bolted for the doorway.

I stopped him just as he reached it.

"Wait." He stopped still, poised and tense as if waiting for the sound of a shot. "One thing, Lee. I haven't told your folks yet who it was that robbed me. Think on that."

He shuddered once and disappeared through the door, closing it behind him.

"Do you think that was the smart thing to do?" Kalb asked. He sounded distinctly doubtful about it.

"Aw, I don't know, Mr. Kalb. I sure don't. But it would

break his daddy's heart to find out Lee was the one that robbed me. I know that much. Lee isn't much, I guess, but his daddy is a fine old gentleman and a close friend to my daddy." I grinned. "I guess I do manage to let things get complicated."

"Say, I forgot to give it to you before, but I have your money here."

"What money? I don't remember you having anything of mine."

"That flyer on Gaspe. Three-hundred-fifty-dollars, offered by Butterfields. It's yours now."

"Oh. I... didn't know."

"It's true anyway." He pulled a bank draft from his shirt pocket.

"You don't have to wait for an inquiry or anything?" I was thinking of the deputy back in Kansas.

"No need. We aren't organized as a state here, you know. As sheriff I could run with a high hand if I wanted to. Lots of leeway if the people upstairs like you." He gave me the draft. I took it without hesitation this time.

"You know, Mr. Kalb, I may have an idea of what I could do with Lee now."

"Oh?"

"Yes sir. I think come morning I will cash this. Use fifty of it to get a horse and a hull for him. And make him carry the rest back to my daddy for me."

Kalb whistled. "Funny. I hadn't noticed before what a fool you are, McMurty."

"Maybe. But I don't think it's all that big a gamble. I think all the wild may have been boiled out of Lee's blood by now. At least this will give him a last shot at being right with himself."

"I admire your guts, McMurty, but I don't think I'd give him another chance to rob me was I you."

"It isn't for him, sheriff. More for the other people involved."

"Including you?"

I shrugged. "Maybe."

"Yeah. Well . . . I'll see you in the morning then. Sure wish you luck."

"Sure. And thanks."

CHAPTER 13

WITH THE HELP OF DIRECTIONS FROM FETCHLER AND FROM two other people I passed on the streets I found my way to Kalb's office the next morning. I was tick-full from breakfast and feeling pretty good. The sheriff was in when I arrived. He was propped in a chair behind a big desk. He looked red-eyed and tired.

"You needn't tell me that Miles never showed this morning," he said by way of a greeting.

"He will," I said. "It's early yet."

"Nope," Kalb said. His tone was awfully positive

The sheriff swung his boots down to the plank floor with a thump. "The night marshal shook me out of bed about four this morning,"

he said. "Someone found Miles in that alley, right on the spot where Gaspe fell. He was cut up pretty thorough."

"Oh, jeez." For some reason that hit me really hard. "That poor, stupid... well, hell!"

"If you'll give me the address I'll write his folks and

make up some sort of lie to tell them. Make out it was an accident or something."

I gave him the address and he wrote it down. "I suppose if he'd owned anything of value you would have a claim on it, but he didn't have so much as a pin of his own."

"I don't suppose you'd know what became of the horse and saddle he had when he rode in here? They were mine too."

Kalb thought for a moment. "I wouldn't know myself, but I think I know someone who might. Want to wait here a little while?"

"Sure."

The sheriff got to his feet. "If anyone comes looking for me, tell them I'll be back directly." I nodded as Kalb got his hat and went out, leaving the door open behind him.

The office was mostly bare save for some notices posted on a board that covered the biggest share of one wall. I read those and admired a set of daguerreotypes on his desk. They showed a plump, gentle faced woman with her hair tied up in a style too severe for the warmth of her expression. And others were views of Sunday-dressed children. The pictures showed several views with several kids in each, but they shook down to four children, one boy and three girls.

Kalb was gone a long time. By the time he returned I'd read every notice on his board and every one of a stack piled in a box on the comer of his desk. Most of them offered cash money for the capture or the death of some man wanted by the law. I was glad when Kalb got back.

"I found out," he said as he came through the door, "but it won't do you much good. My man says he had a good looking sorrel gelding and a new saddle that Jimmy Childress was riding when he left."

"Good," I said. "That's the first new saddle I ever owned. I'll be downright tickled to get it back."

"You don't care how big a chew you cut for yourself, do you?"

"It's so big now a little more won't hurt." I got to my feet and stuck out my hand. "Sheriff, I appreciate all you've done to help. I really do."

He shook with me. "Pulling for Arizona now?"

"Yes sir. If I point my nose west I should find the place, shouldn't I?"

Unless you've got a strange sense of direction, you will. There is a stage road in that direction. Follow it and you'll be all right."

I thanked the man again and left.

It did not take too long to get my things together. I stopped at the express office to send the bank draft on to my father, which still left me with sixty-odd dollars in my pocket. And I did not need as much of that as I thought. Both Fetchler and the man at the livery refused to take payment from me. The charges were taken by Sheriff Kalb, they both said, and that was that. So, I thanked them both and forked the chestnut. I could still get in a half day's ride toward Arizona.

The town was brash and ugly, sun worn and stark. I did

not even know the name of it. I could not understand why men would choose to come to empty country like this. The graze was so poor and the water so scarce a man would be lucky to support a half-dozen beeves to the section.

Not that it was all like this. In some places I'd already seen bluestem and side oats grama deep enough to tickle the chestnut's belly going through it. And there was a little beef here yet. There was sure to be a market for it with the mining camps already here. And the railroads would be along in a few more years, opening the stock-yard markets clear to Chicago or beyond, wherever they were selling high. I could not help wondering when I saw that unclaimed grass how Evelyn would take to the idea of my looking out here again when the time came that I could think of such things again. I guess I was a long way from forgetting my dreams, and I was glad this was so.

I entered the town and found the public stable. The horse had been used hard and fed poorly the last few weeks, so I told the hostler to give him a heavy feed of grain and paid fifty cents up front to see that it was done. The chestnut had lost flesh since I left Santa Fe, and I did not like to see that. A horse should go into the winter butter fat if you want it to come out with more than just hide and bones in the spring.

There was a hotel of sorts in the town, and I carried my gear there and took a room. If you can call it that. I have seen hay ricks with better built walls. The partitions divvying the building into sleeping rooms were not much over six feet tall, just high enough, so you could not see over without standing on something. The bed was a cot with strung ropes for springs. That was the only piece of furniture unless you count the three pegs driven into the outside wall as a wardrobe. For this they charged twenty-five cents, and no meals included. At least they were honest enough to make no pretenses about how secure such a place could be. There were no locks or keys on the doors; instead there was a hook and eye arrangement that could be latched from the inside if you wanted to bother.

I deposited my stuff behind the clerk's desk at the front where at least it might be under his eye. Others had made the same choice before me judging from the stuff piled in the corner there.

I went back to the livery just to check. The chestnut was nose down in a comer trough of oats and barley, so I had no kick there.

Next door to the stable was a hardware store that seemed to specialize in equipment for the prospector or small-time miner. In one comer of the place—which otherwise was filled with contraptions that were beyond my understanding save for the picks and the shovels—was a nicely built and brightly polished bar. It struck me as being a strange combination of businesses, but I guess it made a kind of sense at that.

A man could stop in here to buy any gear he needed and stay to talk mining matters with like-minded fellows. Or he might stop for a snort and see a bit of equipment that he just could not live without any longer. So maybe it was sensible after all.

Anyway, I stopped and ordered a beer, which was flat and tasted somewhat like the color green looks.

"Is the sheriff anywhere around?" I asked after I had suffered through half of my beer.

"Mus' be around somewhere," the bartender said. "I've heard there is such an office, so he jus' gotta be somewhere."

"He's not in town right now?"

The bartender laughed. "I been here since this town was started, an' I've never seen 'im. Don't for sure know who he is or where he'd hang out. Not around here, though."

"How about local law?"

"Naw. No need for it. Anybody gets out of line, why, we get a committee together an' they dispose of things however seems best."

"I never heard of doing things that way."

"It works," he said. "Fill that beer for you?"

"No thanks. I want to go find some supper. What would you recommend?"

"You want a good meal or somethin' to fill your belly 'til the morning?"

"Something good if it can be found."

"Then what you do," the man said, "is get your horse an' head north out o' town about ten miles to them hills you can see up there. You get up in there, see, an' find you a curl-homed sheep or maybe a deer. Shoot it. Whack off a piece. An' cook it yourself to suit your own tastes. That's the surest way." He said it straight-faced.

"Uh huh. And if I decide to stay in town?"

"Pete Marin's place is about all the choice you got. It's that or nothin' around here." He paused and looked me in the eye, deadpan as he could be. "There's some that choose to give up eatin'. Tends to limit their stay in town," he said, "but they generally leave happy when they do go."

"Uh huh. Well, I thank you for your help. You've been most informative."

"Don't mention it," he said politely as he poured himself a beer.

I had already noticed Marin's place. It was next door to the hotel. A big sign at the front said Eats. It had not looked too inviting or I would not have asked that barkeeper for a suggestion.

I went back down that way and pushed inside. Despite the warning I had trouble finding a place to sit. There was but one table in the place, and it ran nearly the full length of the deep, narrow room. Benches lined both sides of the table. Empty plates, piles of spoons and huge bowls and platters loaded with food were spaced down the center of the table.

A fellow I assumed would be Pete Marin was perched on a stool by the front door. He looked sort of like a grease-spattered bird, he was so frail and crusted with stains. Those stains on his apron were of impressive age and variety.

He smiled when I came in. "New here, aren't you," he said. It wasn't a question. "Twenty- five cents. Pay as you enter. Eat all you can stand."

"Why, shoot," I told him while I fished in my pocket for a quarter, "I was told this was the only eatery in town. I expected to be held up for more than that." I gave him the coin.

His smile got bigger and brighter. "If you ain't heard yet, you'll find out soon enough. I'm a God-awful cook, boy. But I ain't stupid. If I charge any less I don't make any money. If I charge any more, someone else will come in here an' run me out of business with some competition. So, I set m' price jus-s-s-s-st right."

I had to laugh with him. He was a likeable cuss.

But he was surely right. He was a God-awful cook.

I finished my meal in a hurry and stuck mostly to the beans, which were less awful than most of the other stuff. And, come to think of it, less expensive. I nodded to Marin on my way out, and he beamed back at me. "See you in the mornin'," he called after me.

I stopped in at the three regular saloons in town and had a beer at each of them, but I could not find anyone who knew where I might find either Bud Terry or Little Jimmy Childress. It seemed Arizona was a good-sized territory. Too big to easily find two fellows in.

After the third horrible tasting beer I gave up and went to bed.

CHAPTER 14

NOW THAT HOTEL BED WAS EVERY BIT AS BAD AS THE FOOD and the drink around this town. It was nothing more than a rope strung cot with too few ropes and a doubled-over ticking mattress to start with. And to top it off, a couple of the ropes had sprung their last. That left some gaps so the impression was not so much that of lying on a bed as of suspending yourself across several crosspieces—something like trying to lie across the branches of a tree. I gave up trying to pretend I was comfortable and spread the mattress on the floor, which was much, much better.

I corked off in no time flat then.

The next darn thing I knew I was sitting bold upright with my mouth hung open ready to holler.

There was a powerful ringing in my ears and the heavy, acid smell of burnt powder was so strong in the confined area that I could actually taste it. I clopped my jaw shut and shook my head. That did not stop the ringing in my ears, but it shook some wood splinters out of my hair.

I ran a hand over my head and brushed out more splinters. The sound of several sets of pounding feet dimly reached me through all the ringing and buzzing going on inside my head.

A man carrying a lamp pushed my door open, bending the thin hook without noticeable difficulty. Another man stood behind him. Both had revolvers in their hands.

"What happened?" He had to repeat it several times before I understood what he was saying. The ringing seemed to be clearing a little bit now.

"I don't know," I told him. Which was the simple truth.

The two men came inside, filling the tiny cubicle. I got to my feet and gathered my shirt and britches and gun belt from the wall pegs. When I had them on I felt better.

I sat on the edge of the bunk frame to pull my boots on. One of the two men pointed over my shoulder and I turned to take a look.

Just above the level of the bunk a hole had been gouged out of the thin board partition separating this from the next room. Long splinters had been blown away from a small hole in the middle. The freshly exposed wood radiated out from that small hole in both directions, running with the grain of the wood.

"If somebody pasted a target on the other side of that wall, I'm going to be real upset about it," I said. One of the two men—the first one I recognized now as the proprietor of the place—went around to the other room.

"No one here," he said, his voice carrying plain over

or maybe through the low partition. "There's flash burns around the hole on this side, though." The proprietor looked thoughtful. "You know, mister, you're kinda lucky," he said. "If the silly son'd had sense enough to look over the wall first, you'd be starting to cool by now."

"You know, you're right." It was not an especially comforting thought. "I don't suppose you saw anyone go running out of here?"

He shook his head. "I was asleep myself." He grinned. "But I'll bet you woke up even quicker'n I did."

"Yeah."

"There's a chunk of firewood hanging over your left ear," he observed.

I located the splinter. He was right. It was most long enough to use for lighting a stove. "Thanks."

"I give special service to anybody that gets shot at in here."

The second man returned. He shook his head. "Not a thing interesting over there," he said.

"There isn't much point in asking, I guess, but was that room rented to anyone tonight?" I asked.

The answer was predictable. "Nope. I try to space out the empties when I can so one fella won't disturb his neighbor too much."

"It's a good thought, but I got to admit I was disturbed."

"Yeah." The two men rumbled around a few minutes more, but there was really nothing they could do. When they decided to go back to bed I grabbed my hat and saddle bags. "Hope you won't be offended," I told the proprietor, "but I think I'll spend the rest of the night somewhere else." I thanked the both of them and eased out the front door. Now that I no longer need it, I was all primed and ready to go for the Dragoon.

I spent the rest of the night on a pile of sacked grain in the livery stable and slept not another wink. It was a long, long night and I had plenty of time to think but I could come up with no good ideas on who might have thrown that shot at me.

Now the why of it was another story. I'd been asking for Terry and Childress. Anyone friendly to them might have decided to do them a big favor. It was a thought of which I did not approve. And like I said, it was a long night.

Come first light I grained and saddled the chestnut. I did not want whoever it was to have a second chance at success.

There were roads leading through town in an east-west direction and another striking out on its own toward the hills to the north. For no special reason—since I did not know where to look except somewhere in this territory—I took the one going north.

Now, though, I was a lot more cautious than I'd ever been before. I might be a bit slow, but I can learn. And having been shot once I was not anxious for a repeat of the performance. So, I rode watching the wagon ruts behind me just as much as the ones ahead.

It was a damn good thing I was, too. Not more than two hours out of the town I was getting some elevation above the town lying those miles behind, and I could see the road for a good distance. About half way between me and the town was a stir of dust. It could have been some honest traveler minding his own business or a few horses running loose, or it might have been a dust devil and therefore nothing at all. Or it might have been the yahoo who took a shot at me. I did intend to find out which and not be so innocent and trusting any longer.

The road was getting into some proper hills now and was beginning to twist and turn to take advantage of the easier slopes. I followed the ruts through a steep-sided rocky cut and turned the chestnut off the road.

With a bit of lurch-and-scramble the long-legged beast made it up a rise that hung above the roadway here. I took the animal well back from the top of the slope and tied him to a lonesome juniper I found there. Then I hiked back to the road and settled myself in a patch of shade at the base of a large rock where I would not be seen by anyone approaching from the town.

I waited a long time without seeing or hearing a thing more than a single paisano bird— roadrunners they called them out here—darting around in search of a snack. Eventually though I heard the soft, rhythmic plop of hooves coming at a trot. The question remained whether the rider was traveling after me or was just traveling.

The man drew abreast of the rock I was sitting by. He did not notice me right off, and I believe he might have passed right on by without ever seeing me there.

Whoever he was, I did not recall ever seeing him before. He was about as medium as a person can get. Medium height. Medium build. Medium brown hair. Nothing outstanding about him at all. He was range dressed but might have been anything at all. He carried a fat bedroll and a rifle in a boot tied to his saddle, and he wore a revolver strapped to his leg lower than most people like to wear them.

I stayed seated and when he was just past I spoke.

"Mornin', neighbor."

By golly, I must have startled him right smart for he really put a stop on the horse he was using. He like to have pulled loose the corners of its mouth. He spun it back to face me.

He saw me and broke into a bashful grin. "Man, you sure put a scare in me there. My thoughts must have been clear off in another country. You got troubles? Anything I can help with?"

Now he sure did seem friendly, offering to help me. And it sure could look like I'd found myself afoot and stopped to rest in the shade while walking toward town. Well, that was just the sort of thing I'd wanted to learn about him. What his intentions were.

"Naw, no trouble," I told him. "Just taking it easy a while. Where does this road go, anyhow?"

He was still smiling pretty. "'Bout seven miles ahead there's a town called Aces."

"Thank you," I told him.

"Any time." He nodded and turned his horse back up the road, and I got to feeling some better about him.

I got to my feet and began the climb back up the hill toward my chestnut.

Behind me I heard a click of rolling metal. Somehow —thank God—I did not mistake it for a shoe striking rock or the jangle of a bit and ring. That smiling fellow had just cocked his revolver.

I spun and dropped. The Dragoon was already in my hand.

A bullet sizzled past and spanged into the rocky ground behind me. I could feel chips of stone or maybe splattered lead peppering my back. The smiling fellow's horse was standing braced and firm under him while he hurriedly thumbed his hammer again. He didn't have that much time.

I snapped a shot at his upper body, and I could see a splash of dust as it took him in the chest. His gun hand sagged, and he triggered one into the ground between us.

He looked at me but did not have the strength to raise the heavy revolver again. He grinned at me and turned loose of the gun. His horse still had not moved.

I holstered the Dragoon and went to him. He was starting to sway in the saddle. I reached up and he leaned to me, so I could lower him to the ground. I laid him out, so he would be as comfortable as possible.

"Sure was stupid of me," he whispered.

"What was?"

"Coulda gone ahead. Waited. Used the rifle. Just goes to show. Don't get impatient. Bad mistake."

"Yeah." But I was feeling icy cold. Good Lord! I'd never thought about him being able to lie in wait for me after I let him pass. It was just blind luck that he'd turned more stupid than me for a moment. I had a whole lot to learn if I was going to stay at this. And stay alive.

"What's your name?" I asked him.

"Doesn't matter."

"You'll want a marker, won't you? Everybody ought to have that much."

"You'd see to that for me?"

"Yes."

"Baker," he said. "Fredrick John Baker."

"All right. I'll see that it's on the marker."

He nodded.

I thought he was gone, but after a moment he said, "You can have my stuff. The horse is a good one.

"I'll take care of him," I promised.

I thought to ask him why he'd shot at me and where I might look for Terry or Childress, but it was too late. By then he was dead.

I tied his horse by the road and went to fetch my chestnut.

CHAPTER 15

THE TOWN TURNED OUT TO BE CALLED ACE, NOT ACES, AND it was much like the one I'd just left except a touch bigger. Big enough to have a barber who doubled as an undertaker when there was need for such service.

I took Fredrick John Baker to him. Baker had twelve dollars in his pockets, and the barber said he would handle the burial for that plus the dead man's gun belt and .36 caliber Colt's revolver, which was all right by me. I added five more to it, so he would chisel a marker out of rock. The barber offered to do it in wood as part of the burial, but I figured Baker would have preferred the stone.

I took both horses to the public wagon yard and saw that they were well fed. Baker had been right.

He'd had himself a good horse there. A red roan with a dark red head and red points, the rest of him mostly light haired. The best thing about him was his build. He had that chunky, solid look of quarter running blood, a deep chest and stout bone in his legs. All in all, he was a whole lot more animal than the chestnut Lee Miles had used to ride.

I left the saddles under a shed by the yard and took both bedrolls, the rifle and my saddle bags with me to the Ace Hotel, which was adjacent to the Ace High Saloon. A room with meals there was a dollar, but after that last hole I'd been in I did not mind paying that price for a proper room with a lock on the door and walls that went all the way to the ceiling.

I felt a little odd doing it, but I went through Baker's bedroll to see if there was anything worth keeping. After all, he had given me his gear. It wasn't like I was stealing from him or anything.

It turned out to be a darn good thing I had not sold the bedroll for the couple dollars such an outfit will bring or swapped it against the cost of a marker for the man. Baker had been one who liked to carry his personal things rolled in his bedding instead of in separate bags like I prefer. Inside the bedding were rolled a new shirt—which fit me quite well—a box of rimfire .44s for the rifle, a silver dress-up belt buckle with a raised floral pattern. And a piece of folded-over calf skin containing two hundred twenty dollars in double eagles.

I wondered if he might have forgotten his bankroll when he gave me his things. That was an awfully large price to pay for a headstone. But there was no way now that I could go back and clear it up. There was no one to ask, no kin that he had mentioned. In the end I decided to do the same with that as I had the bounty money on those others. Take it and send it to my neighbors.

Yet in a way I felt like a paid killer. And I did not want to become a person of that stamp. All I wanted was to get back my neighbors' money— and my own if I could— and go home to Evelyn and to my work. I wanted that more than anything else but could not go home empty-handed so long as there was the faintest chance of regaining some of what had been stolen from me and from the men who had trusted me. I lay awake a long time that night before finally I slept, and my thoughts were not all pleasant ones.

I felt better in the morning, in the light of a new day and with a good breakfast behind my belt. There was an express office in the town served, they said, by a once-a-week stage run. I arranged there to send Baker's money to my father along with a short note asking him to tell our neighbors I was still hopeful I could recover their money. As before, though, I was careful to make no mention of Lee Miles. By now his family would have received word of his death. They did not need more grief.

When that was attended to, I went back to the wagon yard shed for a better look at the two saddles I had left there. Baker's was much better than the old hull Lee had been riding. The man in charge of the yard was a dabbler in assorted merchandise, so I sold him Lee's saddle, the chestnut gelding and Baker's bedroll for twenty-five dollars and my feed charges. He could probably double that in re-sale, but he had the time and the traffic to do it. I would not, and I considered the agreement worthwhile on both sides of the deal.

I saddled the roan and secured my own bedroll and bags to it before I went to do any asking for Terry and

Childress. I wanted no repeats of my experience with Fredrick John Baker. He must have gotten onto me because of the questions I asked.

Of the four saloons in town I chose the brassiest and the loudest to enter first. The place was large, running perhaps sixty-feet each way on a corner lot. Doors faced onto both streets, hung with bead curtains to discourage flies. Inside was a long bar on one back wall. The floor space was taken up by tables and a gambling layout. The center part of the smoothed plank floor was empty, possibly for dancing although no women were evident at this time of morning. The bar was tended, though, and a few early customers were having eye-openers.

I didn't really want anything to drink. When the barkeep came to me I put my questions to him right off. I was surprised by the reaction I got.

The man's face tightened into a harsh, blank stare. "Get out!" he snapped.

"What?"

"We've got no use for gunfighters around here," he said.

"Mister, I don't know what you're talking about."

"You're McMurty aren't you?"

"That's my name, yes, but..."

"Then you'd be the killer we heard about," he said grimly.

"Look, mister, I don't know what all you've heard, but..."

"Shut up! We want no truck with the likes of you or those thieves you want to kill. And I would not point a killer like you at any man. Not even one of them. Now get out of here."

I shook my head and started to explain. But what was the use? He didn't want to listen to anything I might say. He wouldn't believe what he heard anyhow. I clamped my jaw shut and left. I was glad to get out of that place, but somehow the day was not so bright and pleasant as it had seemed a few minutes earlier.

I tried the other saloons but got no information there either. The other bartenders were not so blunt as the first had been. And in fairness to them maybe some of what I was thinking, and feeling was a carry-over from the first place. But the fact remains that I felt something like a scorpion pinned to a board for kids to peer at in fascinated disgust.

The roan was standing patiently on three legs, hip cocked and eyelids drooping. His ears pointed, and his head came up as soon as I took the reins from the post where I had looped them. I flipped the stirrup up and pulled the cinches tight.

"Ahem," a voice said behind me in a poor imitation of a man clearing his throat. It was considerate of him to do it, so he might not startle me, but I'd been aware of the footsteps already. I was not nearly so green now as I once had been. I turned to face him.

The man was a real dandy. Dark gray suit. Tall, light gray hat of good quality beaver, slightly soiled but none the less elegant. Brocade silver-gray vest. Bright yellow cravat. He wore low-top shoes and yellow gaiters. Altogether he was dressed about as fancy as a man ever can be.

Inside the clothes was a fellow approaching old age, large and big-boned and slightly red in the face. His mutton chop whiskers and thick moustache and too-long untrimmed hair were mostly gray with darker flecks showing he must once have had hair as dark as gutta percha.

"Good day, sir," he said in a booming, hearty voice.

"Yes?"

He smiled and continued toward me with his hand extended. "Dr. G.F. Randolph, sir. Physician and pharmacologist."

I shook and introduced myself, wondering what his game might be. "A pharmacologist, you say?"

"Indeed, Mr. McMurty. I have that honor, among certain others."

"You read the bumps on people's heads and know all about them, is that it?"

"Ah no, my lad. You mistake me for a phrenologist, a practice favored by charlatans and others of low moral character. I, sir, am a practitioner of the medical parts specializing in the chemical balances of the human body. A far finer and more honorable calling indeed, Mr. McMurty."

"My apologies, doctor."

He waved the apology aside with a breezy gesture. "Not at all necessary, Mr. McMurty. A simple error easily corrected. A matter of no consequence." He did have a good voice.

The roan snorted, reminding me of what I'd been about to do. "Was there something you wanted, doctor?"

"Yes. Yes indeed, my lad. I shall come directly to the point, sir." He looked slightly pained by the necessity for coming directly to the point. "I, uh, understand you may be traveling through on a northward route, Mr., uh, McMurty." He raised an eyebrow at me.

"I am," I agreed.

"Yes. Good." His forehead wrinkled in concentration. "I am, uh, given to understand further that you are—how shall I put this? —eminently well qualified, to, uh, defend your person against, um, unwarranted assault."

Well, hell. That again. I turned back to the horse and flipped the stirrup back down. "I'm no damn gunfighter," I told him in a flat voice. "Go hire someone else if you want a killing done. Better yet, do it yourself."

I would have mounted the roan but with a cry of "No!" he grabbed my shoulder. I spun, and the big Dragoon was in my hand.

Randolph's eyes walled, and he stumbled backward several steps. He licked his lips and tried to smile.

"You mistake my intentions, Mr. McMurty," he said hurriedly. His hands churned the air between us. "No indeed, sir. No indeed. You mistake me completely, Mr. McMurty."

"Correct me then, Dr. Randolph."

"Yes. Of course." He pointed toward the Dragoon. "Could you . . .? He looked quite pale.

"I guess so." I let the hammer part way down and spun the cylinder around to the uncapped nipple. The color began to come back to his face after I put the gun away.

"Yes. Well now," he said several times, rubbing his hands together. "I absolutely do not want bloodshed, Mr. McMurty. No indeed, sir, I do not. I am a physician, you see, and... No sir, I would not want anyone harmed. Quite the contrary, you see."

"No, doctor, I guess I don't."

"Yes, of course. You see, my, uh, niece and myself are traveling to the north also. We are, uh, examining, the local potential for rendering assistance in the search to achieve an efficacious balance of the body chemistry, you see."

"A medicine man, you mean."

"Precisely sir," he said, beaming.

"And?"

"Yes. Of course. And, sir, we have been told we might encounter road agents or even hostile aboriginals to the north."

"Aboriginals, doctor?"

"Indians, Mr. McMurty. Indians. We have been warned in the most serious terms about this danger, you see."

"I still don't see what this has to do with me, doctor."

"Yes. Well. I, uh, would be grateful if you were to journey northward in, uh, the company of my party. I would feel much more secure, you see. And I would pay you for your trouble, Mr. McMurty. At a rate of, uh, ten dollars per day. In coin, sir."

"How far to the next town, doctor?"

"Five days, I am told."

"Fifty dollars, huh?"

He was beaming again. "In coin. And you are traveling the same road regardless."

I stepped onto the roan. "If you would lead me to your outfit, doctor, we can go any time you're ready."

"Excellent," he said. The good doctor seemed fully recovered from his fright. He turned and marched airily toward the wagon yard. "Follow me," he ordered briskly.

CHAPTER 16

Now I was in for a couple of surprises when we reached Randolph's wagon. And again, a moment or two later.

I have seen a few snake oil peddlers from time to time and know what kind of gaudy, bright painted-up rigs to expect of them. Or at least I thought I did. This, though, was unlike anything I would have imagined beforehand.

The wagon itself was of the ambulance style with a light box built onto a spring frame. It was half-walled and had canvas side curtains that now were rolled up and tied to admit fresh air and light. From atop the roan I could see neatly arranged trunks and boxes along the sides and at the front, crossways to the frame just behind the driving seat, was a padded platform big enough to serve as a bed at night.

The woodwork had a brightly polished shine to it under a coating of road dust. It was painted a dark and dignified maroon, and the wheel spokes were painted and polished to match. On the side was an inset panel that might have been of cherrywood. On this was lettered —it looked to be in gold leaf—a simple statement: G.F. Randolph, M.D.

The team waiting in harness was as nice as the wagon deserved. They looked alike enough to be twins—grays with black points and faint dappling on their broad rumps—and made a spanking pretty team. Both of them were mares. Both were sleek with a layer of healthy fat over their ribs, and their feet were carefully trimmed and shod. No one could complain that Randolph did not tend his animals.

I got the other surprise when a young lady stepped around from the shaded side of the wagon.

Truth to tell, I had been expecting Randolph's 'niece' to be a brash and brassy gal carrying as much paint as the average snake oil man's wagon. But it turned out that Dr. Randolph was not so average in that regard either.

This lady looked like she deserved to be called just that. She was wearing a duster and gloves and a pert little bonnet but even so, I could see how slender and straight she was. Not skinny, mind. There was no doubt, either, about this being a girl. And pretty? High cheek bones and full, moist lips and thin brows curving over ice blue eyes and a halo of jet black curls showing under the bonnet. She'd have been somewhere around my age, and I did not wonder that the doctor would want some protection on the road. In a town he'd never have to worry. There would be such a crowd hanging close that no one could think of being troublesome. The girl came toward us, and I stepped off the roan and yanked my hat off.

"This is Mr. McMurty, my dear. Mr. McMurty, my

niece Jessica Randolph, my youngest brother's only child."

I mumbled something and Jessica Randolph extended her hand to be touched. "A pleasure," she said. "Your name is McMurty?"

"Yes, ma'am. Charles McCown McMurty. And I'm glad to meet you too."

"Mr. McMurty has agreed to ride north with us, Jessica, as a protection from marauders as it were."

"How very kind of you," she said in a silky voice.

I guess I cannot blame him for what Randolph did next. I'm sure he was only thinking to protect the girl from too close an association with an undesirable character, and I can understand that. But I disliked it nevertheless.

"Mr. McMurty is the quick shooting young man we heard of at dinner last night, Jessica. The one who dispatched a ruffian south of the town yesterday."

"Oh!" The ice in her eyes frosted over and she withdrew her hand.

"Are you ready, dear?" Randolph asked her.

He seemed in quite a good humor now.

"Yes. Everything is packed."

"Fine," the doctor said. He helped the girl onto the driving box, unclipped his hitching weights and laid them on the floor beneath the seat. He climbed up beside her and took the reins. "Coming, McMurty?"

"Right behind you, doctor." I got back onto the roan and spun him in behind the wagon. He had the quickest, surest moves I'd ever felt under me and I could not help thinking about what a cutting horse he would make. I sure would've liked to know if he had ever been used for working cows before. But I guess that would have been too much to ask, everything considered. Like where he had come from.

We rattled out onto the road to the north. The tracks climbed a low saddle between two steep sided, rock-strewn hills. As soon as we dropped beyond the saddle it would have been impossible to tell if there was a town or people within ten miles or a hundred. I was already tired of staring at the back of Randolph's wagon, so I nudged the roan and brought him up beside the box on the passenger side.

Jessica Randolph looked just as pretty bouncing along on the seat of that wagon as she had when she wasn't being jostled and jounced. And I had ample time to study her features in profile. She never once turned her head to look my way.

Randolph nodded and smiled and went back to paying attention to the road, which those nice moving mares did not need. Well, that was all right. It was his choice. I went back behind the wagon.

We stopped for nooning in the shade of a high walled bluff where there was a thin patch of grass but no water, which was all right because Randolph had a brim-full keg on his wagon. I found some dry wood and got the fire going while Randolph staked the animals. The girl started to unload boxes of food and stuff from the wagon. When I took them from her to do the carrying she kept her eyes down. But she did accept the help.

It was a mostly quiet meal but a good one, and I enjoyed it thoroughly. Jessica Randolph was a darn good cook. For some reason I felt inclined during the meal to keep reminding myself that Evelyn was an awfully fine cook too. I'd bought a fair number of meals she had prepared for box suppers at dances and such down home, and more than one Sunday I had sat at the Stewart table when she had done the cooking. She can bake a biscuit so light that you'd swear all there is to it is the flavor.

When the meal was done and cleaned up after, I expected we would hitch the team and be on our way again right away. Instead Randolph pulled a pipe and leather tobacco pouch from a case strapped to the dashboard of the wagon. He took his time tamping and firing the pipe.

"No need to hurry, lad," he said when he seemed satisfied with the coal in his pipe. "We'll let the horses graze a while longer before we move."

The girl seemed to find nothing unusual in such a long noon stop. From the same dashboard case she extracted a puff of white lace, some thread and a tatting shuttle. When she spread the lace on her lap to work on it I could see she was making a shawl. It would look downright elegant when she got it done. Such a long rest would appear to be a part of their regular traveling routine. Randolph smoking contentedly and watching his mares graze. Jessica bent over her tatting. For some reason it made me think the more of them, even if he was just a glorified snake oil man.

I had nothing to do, which is a condition I am not accustomed to and do not especially relish. I left them to their pursuits and wandered afoot along the base of the bluff.

The country was stark here and would make poor ground for the raising of stock. Mostly it was bare rock and bare, rocky earth with only irregular clumps of greasewood or salt brush and scattered crowns of coarse dry grasses. The grass was a far cry from the curly mesquite of home, which is so rich I believe it would put fat onto a slab of wood if you could think of a way to feed it. I believe this stuff might have been an impoverished relative of our grama. Whatever it was I did not think much of it as a staple for cattle, and as dry as this country was I doubted that the grass would recover very quickly if you ranged many animals on it.

There was a small overhang above the ground a hundred yards or so south along the wall and when I got close I could see that the underside of the rock was dark. A closer look showed it to be blackened by smoke. It made me wonder, for I would not have expected Apaches to choose a stopping place so close to a road, especially so close to a traveled wagon road.

I wandered over to the outcropping and was surprised to find no ash ring on the ground there. Either someone had done an awfully fine job of hiding his dead fire—which seemed pointless—or it had been an awfully long time since one had been built. I reached up to touch the soot and found that I could not rub any off onto my fingers. It was almost like it was covered with varnish. That must have been really old.

I kicked around in the dirt and found a couple pieces of worked flint and one really nicely shaped arrowhead of an obsidian so perfect it looked like black glass. I rubbed the dust off that one and dropped it into my pocket, just as pleased as I could be though of course it was not worth anything.

Finding that arrowhead took me back some years, and I grinned at the memory. The folks had always accused me of being cross-bred with a pack rat, for I used to carry home all manner of things until the space under my bed was jammed solid with boxes of rocks and old arrowheads and such. I hadn't dragged them out or even thought of them hardly since I was old enough to start working cattle in a serious way, but they would be around somewhere, either still in my room or maybe stacked in a corner of one of the sheds. Mom would remember where.

My thoughts were interrupted by a shout from back toward the wagon. I took off at a run with the Dragoon in my hand.

I was naturally doing some puffing when I broke past the last of the soraggly brush. I looked wildly back and forth for whatever source of danger had prompted that shout. Dr. Randolph was standing beside his team of grays. They were hitched and ready to do some walking —which the good doctor preferred to a trot for some reason. The girl was perched on the driving box. Her tatting had been stowed away again.

Randolph jumped a little when I came busting into sight with the gun in my hand. And I guess it was the second time he'd seen it that day. Then he appeared to realize what I had thought. He relaxed and smiled. "No trouble," he said.

I was still puffing plenty hard. "Good Lord, man," I gasped. "Next time. Just call out easy. Okay?"

"Sure. Sure. Glad to see you are so concerned about our welfare, my boy. Indeed I am."

"Yeah. Well. ..." I let the words die off and went to fetch up my roan. I pulled the cinches tight, feeling foolish and therefore more than a bit irritated. That girl had seen me looking awfully silly and awfully dangerous, both at the same time.

And why should that bother me particularly, I asked myself? I got no good answers, either.

We pulled on north through more rocks and broken hills for what was left of the afternoon and made a late camp at a rock walled pool of water that some thoughtful soul had troubled to clean out and improve for the benefit of those who would follow after him.

Supper was a repeat of dinner and just as good, but again it was a quiet meal. Jessica finally got out of the loose duster she had been wearing all day and truth to tell I was sorrier than ever that she was so set in her opinion of me as nothing but a gunslinger. That was one pretty girl, trim and put together mighty neat.

Her traveling dress was dark, dark blue and very lady-like. High collared. Long sleeved. But fitted close through the waist and, well, upper part of her. I could not see how anyone could possibly stay so crisp and clean-looking after a full day on the road, duster or no, but she had sure managed. Me, I felt like a walking dust lump after trailing that wagon most of the day.

Not that a wagon can raise a tenth of the dirt that a herd of beeves can, but at least when you're out in the lonesome like that you can sluice it off when you come to water. Here that rocked-up water tank looked plenty inviting, but with the girl around all I could do was stare at the firelight reflecting on the pool surface. Sure would have felt good, though.

I gave up the thought and we all bedded down, the girl in the wagon and Randolph under it, me off to myself by the fire.

CHAPTER 17

We went on at Dr. Randolph's slow, deliberate pace for another couple days, and I no longer marveled that he could stay out on the road and keep his team in such fat condition. I could not really complain, though, for the pace was as easy on my roan as it was on his grays, and that tough, red horse began to really bloom.

The country up here was still choppy and bare and could not compare with what I was used to, but I was getting adjusted to seeing so little grass on the ground. And despite my misgivings, whatever this coarse grass was the horses were thriving on it so maybe it could be used to some advantage if a man had enough of it, he could limit and control his grazing in line with the recovery rate of the grasses. For the time being no one seemed to be using it—at least we saw no beef anywhere along the road—but I was willing to bet someone would take up grazing rights on it sooner or later and might be able to make a profit on the venture if he knew his business and watched his grass.

Water was a bit scarce but did not bother us thanks to Randolph's foresight. Whenever we did come to water he topped off the keg even if only a few dippers had been removed since the last time it was filled.

Late in the afternoon of our third day out we came winding down off another of the low hills we were in at the time and crossed a wash to mount the next rise. I was moving in front of the wagon in an attempt to stay out of the clinging dust and crested the rise first. I pulled the roan up short and motioned for Randolph to stop on the slope.

Below me about half way down to a green-scummed pond at the foot of this downslope I could see a brush shelter unlike any I had ever seen before. There was a splash of vivid color showing in the shade under the open-sided structure. On beyond that some movement caught my eye. Sheep. Somehow, on nearly bare ground and in the full glare of sunlight, I had not noticed them until they moved. Now that the doctor's rig was silent the distant bleatings of the woolies rose dimly to me. I turned in the saddle.

"There seems to be a sheepherder's camp down below," I told Randolph. "It wouldn't hurt if you were to wait here while I take a look. I don't see the herder with his sheep."

"Go ahead then." From the dashboard case Randolph withdrew a small, pocket model revolver which he laid uncocked in his lap.

I eased the roan downhill. The horse took it a step at a time, mincing his way carefully. He was a solid thing, though, and did not let any nervousness come through to the saddle. I remembered how he had stood firm during the shooting when Fredrick John Baker was on him.

The thing was, a flock of sheep without a herder standing over them somewhere near could mean some bad trouble coming. I could find almost anything down there, from a dead body to a pack of live Indians. I was on edge the whole way down and was able to ease it only a little by carrying the rifle across my saddle, so it would be ready in case of need.

Nothing stirred except for the sheep. There was no wind to ruffle the brush, no wing-flick or call of birds. The sun heat felt like a weight on my shoulders and I nearly jumped when the sliding tickle of a sweat bead ran down my ribs and startled me.

I came nearer the brush shelter. It was made of sticks and dried stalks of sotol. Under it the color I had seen from above took on form and substance. A blanket wrapped around a human form. I could see no blood. But neither did I see movement.

There was still neither sound nor movement anywhere near. I pulled up by the shelter and sat for a moment before I stepped down and tied the horse to some live scrub. The animal's attention was on the shelter. If anyone else were around the roan was not aware of it, and that would not seem likely.

I knelt and crawled under the shelter. The thin, sun-striped patch of shade gave a sense of enclosure without bringing any real relief from the heat.

The blanket was woven in many colors. It was dusty and worn but still thick and serviceable. I pulled it back from the body it covered.

The face beneath it was thin and drawn and dark brown. A boy's face, just a kid. He had thick, black hair. His eyes were closed. The lids fluttered briefly against the light but did not open. If he was breathing I could not tell it, but he was alive. I laid the back of my hand against his forehead. His flesh was fiercely hot and as dry as old leather. I scuttled backward from the shelter.

I shouted. "Doctor. Dr. Randolph."

I heard a faint, answering, "Yo."

"Drive ahead," I yelled. Within moments his grays topped the rise and I could hear the rattle of their traces. The boy still did not move. He looked close to death.

When the rig was near I walked to the side of the road. Randolph stopped beside me. "What is it?" he asked.

"Are you?" I began. Well, there wasn't much for it except to go ahead and ask and let him feel insulted if he wanted. "Do you really know anything about tending sick people?" I asked the man.

"I do," he said. He gave me an odd sort of look, but he seemed to take no offense at the bluntness of my question. "Is there need for that here?"

"Yes sir. The sheepherder. Just a kid. Mexican maybe."

"What is his trouble?" he asked. He was already rummaging behind him in the wagon.

"Lordy, I don't know. That's why I asked you. Seems sick. He feels awful hot."

"Come along, Jessie," he said. He climbed down from the wagon, a valise in his hand. He handed me his driving tapes. "Tend these horses, boy," he said, but he seemed barely aware that I was there. He and the girl went to the shelter and crawled beneath it.

Knowing by then how Randolph liked to do things I went ahead and blocked the wheels and unhitched the team. I stripped the harness from them and turned them loose wearing hobbles. I did the same for the roan then too. I drifted back toward the shelter though I surely had no knowledge I could add for this occasion.

Randolph glanced up at me. He was totally calm. The girl looked worried enough for the both of them, though.

"He has a high fever, all right," Randolph said. He said some more than might have been in a foreign language for all I could understand of it. And maybe it was. When he saw I did not know what he was talking about he gave a short, impatient little wave of disgust. "The essence of the matter, Mr. McMurty, is that the child is highly contagious. Probably a very good thing we are alone here. He could infect his entire tribe. With no natural immunities they could be wiped out. It has happened before in similar cases."

"That's lucky, I guess."

"Quite."

"But . . . you said 'tribe'?"

"What? Oh. Yes. He's no Mexican. Look at his clothing." Randolph lifted the blanket further for a moment, then tucked the heavy woolen covering tight again around the slim, still figure.

The boy was sure no Mexican. He was wearing a bright red tunic and a loincloth of some sort and high boots made of soft skins. He was sure enough an Indian, but I could not tell of what tribe. I sure hoped he was from one of the tame tribes and not some kind of Apache. I'd never seen an Apache, but I'd heard enough about them to know I did not want to see any, now or any other time.

"Is there a source of water near?" Randolph asked. He was searching inside his bag. The girl had a scrap of cloth and a mostly empty water bag that she must have found already in the shelter. She kept wetting the rag and using it to mop the kid's face. The dry skin seemed to soak up the moisture.

"I can look," I told Randolph. "There's that fouled pond down below. Good enough for the sheep but I don't think I'd drink out of it. Not if I had any choice about it."

"No. Later. For the moment we can use our own. We know it to be clean. Bring a dipper full, that's a good lad."

I got him the dipper of water. He had a little mortar and pestle that he was grinding at, mixing several lumps of dry things taken from small jars. What he ended up with was a red-tinged yellow powder. This he poured into the water and stirred with his finger until it was more or less dissolved.

"Lift him, Jessie. That's it."

They levered the small form until the boy's head was in Jessica Randolph's lap. She steadied him there while Randolph pried his jaw open and tipped some of the discolored water into it. The fluid ran back out the corners of the kid's mouth. Randolph shook his head impatiently.

Jessica Randolph put her hands beneath the boy's neck and pulled so that his head was tilted back. Again, Randolph poured. Some of the fluid ran back out but at least a part of it remained. The girl's duster was becoming wet and stained but if she minded—or even noticed—she gave no indication of it.

Randolph stroked the boy's throat, running his fingers lightly along the under slope of the jaw and down the throat. Within a minute he was rewarded with a swallow, followed by another.

"That's what we want, lad," he muttered. "Again now." He poured more of the medicine between the boy's parted lips. The swallow came more quickly this time. "Good. That's right. Again now," he said repeatedly. His voice was a monotonous, soothing undertone. I doubt he meant the words to have value. It was more like he wanted some form of reassurance to penetrate to the boy's closed-off mind if he should come close enough to consciousness to hear the sounds of comfort.

They continued like that until the cup was empty even though they never once got from the boy a voluntary response to the liquid. Each swallow had to be patiently teased into life by Randolph's deft finger. By the time they were done the girl's duster was liberally splotched with dark, wet stains.

"Good," Randolph said when they were done. He sat upright with a grimace and I realized for the first time how awkward his bent position must have been within that shelter. And he had been at his task for quite some time. His back must have been painfully cramped. He stretched as well as he was able within that space. "Can you continue to hold him?" The girl nodded. She, at least, was able to sit upright near the edge of the shelter.

Randolph peered out to where I was standing. I had

wanted to be able to keep an eye on things around us, but the fact was that most of my attention had been inside that shelter.

"I need your help now, lad. Lots of wood. Water. Doesn't matter if the water is clean or not for this. Something to construct a tent or other closed structure, you see. The child needs to be sweated. Break that fever. No chance at all if we don't."

"Sir? Sweat him? Like the savages do?"

He nodded firmly. "Exactly. Does it sound barbaric to you? Not that I care. It works. Doctors in northern Europe do it also. Just because savages do it, it does not necessarily follow that the practice is inferior. Now. If you could arrange that?"

"Yes sir. Right away."

The wood was easy to come by. The kid, or someone, had piled a good bit of it close to the shelter. And the shelter itself would work for a frame. I went to the wagon in search of a covering, wishing the Randolph's had chosen to drive a bowed and canvas covered rig instead of this much better built vehicle.

I felt like something of an intruder inside the wagon but poked through it regardless. Their bedding I did not think would be heavy enough to contain steam—or for that matter to keep them warm very much longer. It was getting late in the year and quite brisk at night although the season seemed to make little impression on this country during the daylight hours.

Most of the many boxes they carried held bottles of liquids and powders and crystals. Presumably this was the stuff Randolph used to balance the body chemistry.

Sure, it was! And when someone was sick, really needed help, the good doctor fell back on some Indian remedy as primitive as that boy he was 'treating'. Sure, he was! Well, it was what I'd expected anyway. And I didn't have anything better to offer the kid than what Randolph and Jessica could do for him. I kept looking.

What I finally ended up with was so damn obvious I was peeved with myself for not noticing it right away.

The side curtains of the wagon were just what the doctor ordered. Literally. They were nailed in place at the top with painted and polished tack strips there to keep the canvas from tearing loose from the staples. I pried the strips loose carefully and pulled the staples, so I could put Randolph's wagon back together after the boy was dead.

The water turned out to be no real problem either, but if the kid had been drinking much green, slimy, sheep-fouled stuff as this it was no wonder he was so sick. The water hole was a shallow pond no more than a dozen feet across. It had to be a seep, self-renewing, or it could not have held water in the constant dry heat, especially with a large flock of sheep—several hundred of them anyway—drinking from it several times daily.

I filled four of Randolph's biggest pots with the nasty stuff. It would do for making steam, and the pots could be scrubbed clean later.

I got the fire going good and brisk and set rocks in the flames to heat for the steam making. Even if I didn't hold with the idea I could see that it was done right.

CHAPTER 18

THAT OLD MAN DARN NEAR RAN MY LEGS OFF THAT afternoon and on into the night. Heat rocks. Bring more water. Find more wood. Haul those rocks out; heat them afresh. More rocks. We need more water, boy. Don't slow down. Get more wood. Heat those rocks again. By gosh, I was beginning to wonder if he would ever quit.

Jessica was having it just as rough, though. Randolph took no more pity on her than he did on me. She spent the whole time right under there with the kid, holding him and crooning to him and throwing water on the rocks and breathing that hot, moist air right along with the boy. It couldn't have been easy for her. She never said the first word of complaint. I got the idea Randolph wouldn't have quit, or let her quit, even if she had.

I guess I noticed when it got dark, but it did not make all that much of an impression. Just that it became harder to find wood. The generous supply beside the shelter had been used up in no time, and Randolph had not been about to settle for anything less than a huge fire. I tried to tell him such a fire was likely to draw company and maybe unwelcome guests at that. It made no difference to him that I could see. None at all.

"We'll take that as it comes," he said. "This is more important."

So, I went back to my fetch-and-carry work. And the girl kept on under the shelter. And the doctor? He sat comfortably between the fire and the shelter, smoking his pipe and seemingly enjoying the night to the fullest. He certainly showed no excitement, even while he was insisting how important this was. Didn't do much either beyond issuing his instructions to Jessica and to me.

The night was half over with and I was really dragging before there was any change. I was lugging more water up from the seep when someone shouted above me. I dropped the pots and ran heavily upward.

Jessica struck a sweat-runneled face between two draped side curtains. A huge grin hid the tiredness in her eyes. "It broke," she said with delight. "He's running sweat and squirming all over my lap."

Randolph smiled. He reached forward to push a wet rope of hair out of her eyes. "Of course," he said smugly. "What else would you expect?"

"It's marvelous. Really." The tiredness seemed to be gone all of a sudden. "Uncle George?" "Yes?"

"That's why you wanted me in here, isn't it? So, I could see how wonderful it really is, just like you told me it would be, when you talked to me all those times."

"Naturally," he said. He was still sounding smug. He looked at me and smiled. "She'll make a fine nurse, this girl. She has a lot to learn, but she'll be just fine." He seemed downright cheerful. And not at all surprised.

"Good Lord!" I said. "You really are a doctor."

"Of course, I am. I told you so. Whatever else could you have thought?"

"But. . . back in town. You said... You told me you were traveling around peddling, like, patent medicine stuff. You know. A drummer. A medicine man."

Randolph threw his head back and rocked with laughter. "Oh dear," he said when he could speak again without interrupting himself with peals of renewed laughter. He wiped his cheeks and eyes. "Oh dear. Is that what a medicine man is out here? Oh my, no." He chuckled to himself again. "I thought... you meant a man of medicine, you see. A drummer?" It set him off to laughing yet again. "I am a researcher, my dear boy. A physician. Traveling to collect samples and the experience of others. I try to expand the profession's knowledge of herbs and other chemicals. To achieve an efficacious balance within the body, you see. Just as I informed you earlier." He kept on chuckling to himself. Shaking his head with his amusement.

Well, I shook mine some too. "And I had you pegged for some new kind of snake oil man. Good grief. A real doctor." No wonder the wagon and the girl had seemed all wrong for this kind of thing. That kind of thing, rather. Not theirs. From inside the shelter I could hear the girl laughing too. A research doctor, for crying out loud. A real one.

"Will the boy be all right?" I asked in an attempt to

take their interest off my stupidity. But I still felt awfully foolish.

"I believe so," the doctor said. "Once the fever has broken the greatest danger is past. Undisturbed rest, fluids and nourishment should complete the task." He gave me a look of quiet amusement and added, "And, of course, a dose of Doc Randolph's magic elixir, a derivative from the glands of several species of tropical snakes."

I could not help grinning at him. "Guess I earned that."

"Yes." Randolph sighed and knocked the dottle from his pipe. "Now I suppose in fairness it should be my turn to do some work." He got to his feet and made for the wagon. "I trust that fried pork, boiled rice and pork gravy will suffice," he said over his shoulder.

My oh my, but that was so. My stomach did a few flip-flops at the mention of food. I had completely forgotten about supper and here it was close to breakfast time. Fried pork sounded just fine.

And Dr. Randolph turned out to have more than enough competence for that job, too. He could make a better gravy than any trail cook, or most women I've known. I don't know about the others, but I enjoyed every mouthful that came my way and then laid down and was lost to the world until the sun was nearly fully up again.

The girl was awake when I raised my head come morning. She was sitting beside the still live coals of last night's big fire.

"There is coffee ready," she said in a hushed voice when she saw me stir.

"Thanks," I said. "Sounds good." I put my hat on and shifted closer to the pot. One of the side curtains had been pulled aside to let air into the shelter. "Is the boy all right?"

She smiled. "Sleeping comfortably. It is really something, isn't it? To snatch someone back who has been so close to death. It is really wonderful." There was a sense of wonder, of awe, in her tone.

"Yes, it really is. You hadn't seen it before then?"

She shook her head. "First time." She poured a cup of stout coffee and handed it to me, handle first. "That must be why Uncle George insisted I come along on this trip."

"I sort of had the idea y'all travel together all the time."

"No, this is the first time I've ever joined him. He is a lecturer at the university, but he makes trips like this every year looking for new substances to work with. Sometimes in this country and sometimes to other parts of the world. He goes all over. This time ... well... I think he asked me to come as a sort of consolation, so he can convince me to become a nurse. He tells me I would be good at it. I wanted to go to college. Daddy wouldn't hear of that. He thinks just because I'm a girl it would be a waste to send me to college. Uncle George wouldn't think that way. You never saw two men more different than Uncle George and my father. Oh!" She shut up then and got a funny sort of look.

"Something wrong?"

"I... No. Nothing." She shook her head firmly and her hair, unpinned, flew.

"Something is. Tell me."

"I couldn't. It wouldn't be ... polite."

"Um, like that, is it? I wouldn't mind. Really. But I would like to know what shut you off. I mean, I don't think I just did anything that should upset you, but if I did I'd like to know about it."

"You didn't. Honestly," she insisted quickly.

"Well then?"

"It's just..." She dropped her eyes. "No. I shouldn't say anything more."

"Please."

"Well." Her eyes were still down. "It's just that I've never talked with anyone at all like you before. I mean, I didn't really know there are such people. I thought gunfighters and . . . killers . . . were just made up. Like in dime novels or something. And here I am, chattering away ... with you ... at the crack of dawn, out in the desert with no one but our own little group for who knows how many miles in any direction. It is just . . . real strange. You know?"

What do you say to something like that? A gunfighter. A killer. Yeah, girl. Thanks a lot. I wondered if I could ever explain it to her... if she might learn to understand.

"Look, Miss Randolph. Your uncle is a wonderful man. After last night I guess I'd have to say he is a pretty fine doctor, too. But I think he gave you a wrong idea about me. You see...." Well, I tried to explain it to her. Why I was here and what I was doing and—most of all— that I was and am NOT a killer. That I am a cowman, plain and simple. I hoped some of it got through to her.

She was quiet for a minute when I was finished. She started to speak. I really would have liked to hear what she was going to say. She was interrupted by a choking sort of groan from the boy under the shelter. The girl scrambled toward him immediately, all else forgotten.

In a moment her head and shoulders reappeared at the opening to the shelter. She had a smiling, almost an angelic, look to her so I knew there was nothing to be worrying about.

"Can you talk to Indians?" she asked excitedly. She looked really happy.

"Same as you can," I told her. "In English."

"Darn!" she said with force. From the look of daring in her expression when she said it, I got the idea that was quite a cuss word for the likes of her. "He's mumbling something, you see. I was so hoping you could speak Indian."

I had to laugh at her. "Miss Randolph, there must be a hundred different kinds of Indians and just about every tribe has their own language, the same way Americans and Mexicans talk different. Why, we don't even know what tribe this boy belongs to."

She said, "Oh," in a very small voice. She brightened. "In that case how about handing me that pan by the coffee pot? He must be hungry."

I got the pan for her and glanced into it while I handed it across. It was a thin sort of bean soup with nothing but a couple scraps of salt pork in it to give it flavor and strength. I don't know about the preferences of small Indian boys, but if I'd been that sick I know what I would've been craving. Fresh meat and lots of it. Fried in tallow if I could get any. But I gave her the pan anyway. Doctor's orders and all that.

She had the kid's head in her lap, so she could spoon

feed the watery broth into him. He didn't seem real delighted with it, but then he'd been a pretty sick boy. And maybe Indians don't show it when they like something. I wouldn't know.

Just in case I'd had the right idea about what the kid needed, though, I caught up the roan and threw my saddle on him. I pulled the rifle from its boot and went to look around a bit.

I rode down past the sheep. They were still bunched together and seemed to be doing all right for themselves finding food and water. They are supposed to be even dumber than cows—and that can be plenty stupid—and to have no fight in them—which you sure cannot say about long horned cow critters—but I did not know enough about them to know what, if anything, I should do for them. There had to be some reason why there was always a herder with them day and night, but I did not know what it might be.

I was hoping to find a tender antelope or maybe a fat doe deer, but I went several miles without seeing the first sign of game. It turned out I hadn't been looking in the right places. About three miles from camp I heard a rattle of rocks on a jagged bluff face above me. There were three brown desert sheep there staring at me from between the curls of their horns. They would do nicely, I figured.

The Winchester rifle came comfortably to my shoulder—I had handled the '66 model before— and I pegged the front sight low on the shoulder of the nearest sheep. It came tumbling down with the first shot, and the others sprang away out of sight, leaping easily along a bare face where I wouldn't have thought a spider could cling.

I cut the saddle of fresh meat from the young ram and wrapped it in a square of hide for carrying. I headed back for the camp. When I got there the doctor was awake.

"Good morning, my lad," he said cheerfully as I dismounted and handed the meat to the girl.

"Mornin', doctor. I brought some fresh meat for our breakfast. It's probably the sort of thing the boy would like too. Him being an Indian, you see."

I expected some argument. Instead Randolph looked thoughtful for a moment. He said, "That would be the sort of thing he would like, wouldn't it? How would you fix it?"

"Oh, I suppose I'd just whack off a piece of it, push a stick into it and dangle it over the fire. Something like that."

"Jessica, if you please?"

The girl pretended to shudder. "It sounds positively gruesome. But I have to admit he didn't care much for my broth." She got a knife and unwrapped the meat, paying attention to the fleecy hide while she did so. "What is this, anyway?"

"Curly horn desert sheep."

She and the doctor both gave me odd looks. "What's wrong?"

Randolph looked rather amused. "How far did you ride to find the animal?"

"About three miles each way. Why?"

He grinned and raised one arm, pointing one long,

tapered finger downhill toward the several hundred head of woolies grazing there.

"Aw, shoot," I said. "I mean . . . they aren't food. They're stock!" It made perfectly good sense to me. But I don't think they ever did see the difference.

CHAPTER 19

I BELIEVE THAT KID ATE A GOOD HALF OF THAT CHUNK OF meat I'd carried in. He never smiled or made any other sort of fuss to show that he was pleased, but he surely did pack his belly full. It was hard to believe that one skinny kid could eat so much.

Dr. Randolph and Jessica marveled at him as much as I did. The doctor even dragged a notepad out of his case and wrote down something about the boy and how he could put meat down when he'd been so sick. The girl would have been too busy for the taking of notes. She was the one who was cooking and carrying it all.

"Looks like the boy's cured, doctor. I have to give you credit for it too. I sure wouldn't have thought it from the way he looked just yesterday," I told Randolph that afternoon. "I think we should be moving along now that he's better."

The man looked at me like I had insulted him. "Cured? The child is a long way from being cured, Mr.

McMurty. He needs rest. Fluids. Food. I thought I told you all this last night."

"Yes sir, you did, but... I hope you understand the seriousness of staying here longer. You hired me to protect you. That is just what I am trying to do, doctor. And we have been making ourselves kind of conspicuous, with the big fire last night and my rifle shot today. It wouldn't be wise to stay any longer."

Randolph gave me a no-nonsense shake of his head. "Utterly impossible, my boy. Beyond consideration entirely."

"Look. Doctor. You don't know this country. I don't know it all that well myself. But I do know if there are any hostiles around, we are making it awfully easy for them to find us. Why, for all we know, that boy's relatives might be hostiles themselves. Someone is sure to come around soon to collect him and check on those sheep. We can leave him with food and water here, and his friends can take over caring for him as soon as they arrive. He's well enough for that, doctor. You know he is."

"I know absolutely no such thing, Mr. McMurty. I do know that that child in there," he jerked his thumb harshly toward the shelter, "has been desperately ill. I do know the quality of care he continues to need. I do know that he would not receive that care from his savage relatives, even if they were to join him within five minutes of our departure. Why, he might still infect them if they were to join him at this stage." He looked downright stubborn about the whole thing. "And I do know that I will not, under any circumstances whatsoever, leave that child's side until he is capable of resuming normal activity. In the meantime, I appreciate your concern, but I could not possibly take your advice." He smiled, a benign and patient look. "After all, young man, that is the purpose of one's becoming a physician. To tend. To heal. I could not do otherwise."

By golly, the man meant every word of it, too. He wasn't trying to twit me the least bit. And this was the guy I had taken for a damned low-life snake oil man. How wrong could one man be about another?

About all I could do in a situation like this would be to protect them the best I could. I checked my Dragoon to make sure my percussion caps were fresh and dry. At a time like this I'd have liked to have had that sixth chamber loaded and capped, but there would have been no point in loading it. Aside from it being safer to carry the hammer down on an open nipple, you just can't fire the sixth shot out of one of those cap and ball Colts. There is no recoil shield at the cut-out part of the frame where you place the caps on the nipples, so the recoil of the first shot throws that sixth cap off onto the ground if you try to load it full up.

I emptied the magazine of the rifle and cleaned the powder residue from the barrel—it having been fired so recently—and loaded it back again, adding one to the magazine to make up for the one I'd fired at the sheep. And that was about all I could do to get ready in the event we had any trouble.

Jessica was busy cooking the last of the meat, and Randolph was busy contemplating the depths of his pipe. I don't know where he got his tobacco, but he must have selected it for sheer strength of odor. Boy, could he set up

a stink around him. Me, I took the rifle and walked off
from camp aways to do some looking.

Now I do not know too much about Indians and
fighting and warfare and such, but I figured I could make
up in common sense for a lot of what I lacked in experience. I've found that a man can generally get along with
new needs if he will just sit down to some serious
thinking and let his common sense do the work for him.

Anyway, what I was wanting to do now was walk a
wide circle around the camp looking for ways someone
might be able to creep up on us without being seen. It did
not seem likely that Indian trouble would come open and
easy to handle the way it would with white men. Right
now, though, I would've welcomed some white company
in almost any form. Except maybe for Bud Terry or Little
Jimmy Childress. Right now, I did not even want to find
them. Not until I knew the doctor and his niece were safe
at the next town.

My walk proved one thing. The Indian kid or
whoever else might have placed him here with the sheep
had been pretty clever about choosing the spot for his
shelter. The crest of the hill above was too far for bowshot
and from all I'd heard of Indian marksmanship it was too
distant as well for a serious rifle attack.

The ground around the camp was mostly bare, the
slope even and open to the eye for more distance than I'd
realized until I paid special attention to it. It was a thing
that had been open for me to see from the moment I had
arrived, but I had not been thinking then in terms of
defense from attack. Someone else surely had given it
some thought, though. From here the boy could guard

his sheep and himself very nicely. No doubt the shelter was put here in spite of the roadway, not because of it. I felt a lot better after I'd had my walk.

Randolph was grinding another powder when I got back to the fire. He mixed it with water and gave it to Jessica with a little nod toward the boy. It looked like he was using his knowledge but was giving her the task—and the rewards—of effecting the cure. I sat beside him and helped myself to a cup of coffee.

"You still insist on staying here do you, doctor?"

"As much as ever," he said. He began packing his tools and jars back into the bag. "The child is responding beautifully, lad. To leave him now would be to put it all to waste."

"Would you humor me about something, then?"

"If I am able. Of course."

"Well, you should be able, doctor. Not comfortable, mind you, but able. What I think we should do is to keep watch at night as well as during the day. One of us awake all the time. And I need to be the one awake, the second half of the night. It isn't that I want to grab off the first sleep, but I've talked with some fellows back home who run their cows on the west Texas frontier. There are Lipans out there, and I've heard it said they are kin to the Apache tribes here and in New Mexico. Anyway, those fellows should know. They say the most likely time for the Lipans to jump a camp is just before full light. I want to make sure I'm the one awake then."

Randolph considered this and nodded. "All right. We can do that if you wish."

"I can sit up part of the night too," Jessica said quickly.

She was behind me although I hadn't heard her return from the boy's shelter.

"Nonsense, child," Randolph chided her. "This sort of thing should be left to the men."

"Nonsense yourself, Uncle George. If I can sit up with a sick boy I can sit up with my eyes open for a few hours. If I see anything I don't have to do the fighting for you, you know. I could simply give Mr. McMurty a shake."

"It makes sense, doctor. I don't want to be telling you what to do, but I've spent a good many sleepless nights singing to bunches of spooked critters. It begins to wear on one after a while."

"Humph. Had I had any foreknowledge of this sort of thing I believe I should have gone to Italy this year. Too late for that now, of course. I suppose under the circumstances, I must permit you to participate, Jessica. But only the first third of the evening, mind, when you can also tend the boy. Then you shall waken me. And I in turn shall waken Mr. McMurty here. That should allow adequate rest for all until the boy is well."

"How long are we talking about, doctor? Until we can leave?"

Randolph shrugged. "What doctor could predict this with any hope for accuracy? One person might require a month for recuperation. Another only a week. How can I know?"

"I'd like to put a limit on it, doctor. You're tempting the fates if you don't. We should have pulled out this morning."

"We already discussed that, Mr. McMurty. Besides, the rest will be good for the horses. Don't want to over-work them, you know."

"Doctor, their biggest danger from you is starvation."

"Come again, sir? Starvation?"

"Yes sir. They're in danger of you moving so slow that they'll overgraze the area around them and plumb starve to death because of it."

That struck him as being right funny. But I wasn't far from being serious about it.

We began keeping a full time watch that night, Dr. Randolph and I turning in early, so we could be wide awake and properly rested when we needed to be. It had to be the hardest on Randolph, though. In spite of standing a regular watch Jessica got to bed at pretty much a normal hour and could sleep straight through until morning. I just got up a couple of hours earlier than I normally would and could sack out early to make up for it. Randolph, though, had his rest broken right in the middle, and him the oldest and least resilient among us. Still, I could think of no better way to arrange it and had to let it stand like that.

I suppose you could say the effort was mostly a waste when it turned out there were no wild Indians creeping up on us that next morning. But in a way it was not because I learned something kind of interesting in that gray, pre-dawn time. I sat feeling the bone-searching chill that seems to come along with the pale, thin half-light before the coming sun throws splashes of color into the eastern sky. I shivered and huddled close to myself under the blanket I had wrapped around my shoulders.

I sat there and watched, head turning in an effort to see in all directions at once, rifle across my knees, straining for vision until my eyes felt grainy. Slowly, so very slowly, the color came into the sky to my right. Purple and red and pink and fawn and finally the bright, clear blue of the full light. No Indians. No stealthy hints of motion.

And darned if I didn't feel sort of cheated.

I had gotten all primed for it. I had felt so sure. All that worry about the big fire the night earlier. The worry about the shot I had fired within a few miles of camp. The discussions with Dr. Randolph, telling him he should leave behind him the boy he had accepted as his patient and his responsibility.

All that and now the damned Apaches were nowhere around.

Like I said. I really felt sort of cheated. When I should have felt relieved. It made not a lick of sense. It interested me, if only for that reason. I should not have felt disappointed about anything on such a morning. In a way that worried me.

Well, I guess I shouldn't have been disappointed or worried, either one. It was my timing that was off, not my thoughts about the danger we were in.

They came the third morning I was sitting there wondering and waiting and shivering under my blanket. I really would've preferred more of that disappointment.

CHAPTER 20

IT WAS NOT AT ALL WHAT I EXPECTED WHEN THEY CAME. I had talked with fellows who'd fought the Lipans and with a few who had come up against the Mescaleros. Every one of them talked about how those Indians would creep in close without being seen and suddenly leap up and attack from a range so close they said a person couldn't hardly believe it.

Not these fellows. Just before sun-up they appeared at the crest of the hill above us, mounted on paint-daubed horses and standing in plain sight. If they intended this to be menacing they were doing a pretty good job of it. But in truth I guess I did prefer it to the idea of a surprise attack from close range.

I stood and hefted the rifle in my hand to make sure they could see it. One of them—I counted eleven in all— held his rifle into the air. The others did the same.

Those fellows I had talked to were wrong about that too, then. They had said most Indians still carried bows and arrows, that few of them owned rifles. Not this crew. This bunch was well supplied with firearms.

I went to the wagon and roused Dr. Randolph and the girl. "We have company, doctor. Get your gun. Jessica, better get under the wagon."

The girl wasted no time. She slipped over the side of the wagon and into the space her uncle had just vacated. It was too late now, of course, but I realized then that I could and should have put a piled rock barricade around the underside of the wagon frame. It would have been a whole lot safer for Jessica.

The Indians were still at the top of the hill. They hadn't moved except to lower their rifles back to waist level. I wondered what they were waiting for.

"Doctor, why don't you get to the other side of the wagon and keep a watch below and to the sides. Those ones up above are making such a show that I wonder if they're trying to keep our attention on them while something else happens elsewhere."

"All right," he said. His voice was as calm and as normal as if I'd just asked him to hand me the coffee pot. He sure was not one for going to pieces in a tight. "Shall I shoot if I see anyone there?" he asked.

I gave it some thought, still watching the motionless forms above. "No," I told him finally. "Not unless they shoot first. Or if you believe they are about to. If you see anything, tell me."

"Very well." He walked unhurriedly to the downslope side of the wagon and leaned against it. I had to admire the man.

Above us the band of Indians continued to sit, staring down at our camp but making no hostile moves yet. I would not have minded if they had waved bye-bye and ridden away.

They made a brave show of it, I would have to say. Under less threatening circumstances the sight would have been downright interesting.

The first rays of sunlight slanted across them from the left, making them stand out in bold relief against the half lighted sky like so many brightly colored statues. For the first time I understood why Indians are called 'red' men. I have seen enough tame ones along the cattle trails, especially up in the Nations, but they had all looked merely drab and brown and dirty to me. These warriors, though, in the early sun looked as if they had been cast from some hard, shiny, red-tinged metal.

Bundles of bright-dyed feathers fluttered from their rifles and the trappings of their ponies. There were few articles of clothing among them, but what they did wear was of stark white and brilliant blues and yellow and scarlet. I was surprised, but I could see no paint on them.

I had always heard that war parties painted themselves.

The ponies were nearly as wildly colored as their riders. Mostly they were paints with splotches of white prominent on their front quarters, but two were tough looking duns. They were small, close coupled beasts and lightly built. I doubt that a single one of them would have gone eight hundred pounds and most would have been closer to seven hundred. Unlike the warriors, they had been painted, streaked with vermillion and yellow clay. The Indians used no regular bridles on them, controlling them by a single cord that looked like it was tied around their jaws without benefit of a bit of any kind. I'd never seen a rig like that before. I wondered how well it would work when they needed some stiff control on their mounts, like a hard stop.

All of which was real impressive from the viewpoint of a spectator. But I had my doubts about us remaining as interested spectators much longer. I kept wondering what they were waiting for. They sure were in no big hurry about it.

The one in the middle—he was dressed no different than the others—kept swiveling around to look behind him. Directly he waved to someone or something back on the other side of the hill and a minute or two later a twelfth one rode up to join them, stopping beside the one in the center for a talk. In a few more minutes the process was repeated and there were thirteen of them staring down at us.

"Looks like they might've had some scouts out," I said over my shoulder. "If they're going to do anything this might be the time." Randolph grunted, and I could hear the girl shifting around underneath the wagon.

The Indian in the center hollered something to the others. Part of the sound carried down the hill to us. They all wheeled their horses and held their rifles into the air, yelping and shouting so we could hear it plain. The ponies plunged back down off the crest and out of view.

They left nothing visible behind them, not even a haze of dust hanging in the air. But they did leave behind an odd feeling, a sort of emptiness I suppose you might say. It was like something being there that you knew was really not. Or, more, like something was missing that you felt should be there. Whatever, it was awfully quiet and still when they left. I could hear the deep, regular breathing of the Indian sheepherder kid under the shelter and the sound of grass stems tearing as the horses cropped the sparse bunches near the wagon. Maybe I should have relaxed, but I was more on edge than ever now.

Dirt and rock crunched under foot as Randolph came around the back of the wagon toward me, and I could hear the girl stirring again underneath it, fixing to crawl out, probably. I do not know why but I waved at them behind my back and muttered, "Stay there." They didn't argue. The noises stopped.

I hefted the rifle, and it felt good in my hands. It was a comfort to have it there. I thumbed the hammer back—I must have checked three times already to make sure there was a live shell in the chamber—and knelt facing upslope. I still did not know what I was waiting for. I wanted a drink but was not willing to turn and get it. It was yet much too early for the heat of the sun to have any weight to it, but I felt like it did anyway.

For what seemed a long time there was no noise except the breathing of the boy and the chew and shuffle of the horses. A bead of sweat collected somewhere near my hat and ran down my cheek. The feel of it was so acute I could practically see the way it looked. Nervousness, I guess. I was plenty keyed up.

They were back. No sound. No warning. No yelling or carrying on. They simply were there again, standing out again bright and hard against the clean, pale blue of the sky. They sat upright, rifles lifted and bundles of feathers streaming in the wind. The ponies were already at a hard run when they crested the hill, nostrils flared and reaching for air. They dipped and darted, scrambling for footing on the uneven ground, but the riders appeared not to notice. The Indians rode upright and steady no matter how the ponies moved.

The rifle came up to my shoulder and fitted snug against my cheek. I lined the sights on the lower chest of a man immediately above me and waited, finger curled against the trigger but no yet pressing against it.

They must have seen me. As soon as my rifle came up they began to yell. I could not tell if the yipping, shouted noises were words or were only so many sounds meant to bolster their own spirits or perhaps to strike fear in us below. I remember wondering that, even at the time.

The one in the middle pointed his rifle downhill, holding it in one hand and not trying to draw careful aim, which is something you cannot really do anyway from the back of a horse running on poor footing. He fired, and I heard the brief, angry sizzle of a bullet passing close overhead. The others were quick to fire after he did.

Well, that answered that. It wasn't some kind of playful bluff. I'd sort of hoped it was.

I let my finger curl back against the trigger. The rifle cracked and jumped against my shoulder. The Indian jerked backward, his rifle spinning into the air. He straightened and then slumped forward and tumbled off his pony head first. I did not think he would be getting up again.

The others were bent forward over their ponies' necks

now, offering much less of a target of themselves. They continued firing, their bullets spattering into the ground well downslope of the camp, occasionally striking to the front and whining past with a vicious buzz. They dusted me with thrown dirt but did not get a solid hit. Some of their bullets thumped into the wood of the wagon box. I hoped Jessica Randolph was all right under there.

Riders and ponies stood out now against a backdrop of smoke and churning dust and nearly obscured sky. They swept toward us and I snapped a shot at the closest, missing the rider and drawing a splash of blood on the white neck of the pony.

I crabbed quickly sideways to be at the back of the wagon. In truth I was not thinking right then about protecting Jessica with my body between her and the bullets. I did not want to be ridden down by those racing ponies. The bulk of the wagon would make them veer aside.

I jerked at the lever of the rifle and took another shot as they rushed past. The Indian was clinging on the far side of his pony but hadn't gotten low enough. I got lead into his body and he fell. The others were already past, and I could hear Randolph's little pistol talking. I worked the lever and put a finishing shot into my downed Indian before he could scuttle into the protection of what little brush there was around him.

The whoops and yells of the Indians were coming from further away now, and the doctor had quit shooting. I stepped around the wagon. Below us the Indians were dashing through the flock of sheep. They fired wildly into the scattering woolies as they rode. The dust was even heavier now, the sharp hooves of the sheep adding to it. It nearly hid the dead and bleeding sheep and even the running horses of the war party.

At the bottom of the hill they swung to the right along the foot of the slope. I tried a long distance shot at one of them quartering away and I believe hit him. He didn't come loose of his horse, but he did seem to flinch so maybe he was tagged. They kept going and I threw a few more rounds after them, not with any hope of hitting anything but to let them know we would not be taking the raid casually.

When I turned the doctor was kneeling by the wagon. "Is she all right?" I asked him.

"Of course," the girl snapped at me.

"Good. But you stay right there, hear? They might try us again."

"Do you really think so?" Randolph asked.

"I honestly don't know, but I wouldn't take a chance on it. You'd better reload just in case."

He nodded and began fumbling powder and balls into the little revolver that looked so out of place in his hands. It was pretty good advice, so I took it myself and thumbed fresh shells into the long magazine of the Winchester. This business of using metal cartridges sure beat loose powder and ball, and I began to give some thought to maybe having the Dragoon fixed so it would handle the .44 rimfire cartridges too. I'd heard there were gunsmiths making such conversions. It would be a thing to look into one of these times.

I had forgotten about the Indian boy, but Randolph hadn't. He thrust his pistol, flask and a pouch holding balls and caps at me with a quick, "If you wouldn't mind," and went to the brush shelter. He crawled inside, and I finished his loading.

"Jessica. Hurry! Fetch my bag." The doctor's voice was strong and clear and calm. The urgency was strictly in the words. None at all crept into his tone. The girl popped out from under the wagon and reached into it for Randolph's bag.

"Miss Randolph, you'd best stay under there. Those Indians might come back."

It seemed a reasonable enough warning to me, but the girl did no more than send an indignant glance my way. Randolph said, "Hush, McMurty. This boy has been shot." I guess that said it all as far as he was concerned.

Me, I was still worried. Those Indians might well come back.

CHAPTER 21

I BELIEVE WE HAD MADE THOSE INDIANS MAD. THEY CAME at us twice more before it was even noon. These other times, though, were not so bad as the first had been. They seemed darn well aware of what could be done with one rifle, and they no longer pressed their attack so close, preferring instead to rush and deliver a regular storm of fire but flaring off before they were in range for shooting with any certainty—which is a lot closer than most fellows like to admit. What I think they were hoping for would be a lucky shot amongst their fusillade to put my rifle out of commission, so they could close in and finish the work. Thank goodness they were rotten lousy shots themselves, at least from horseback.

I don't know where the people like Dr. Randolph— and Jessica too, for that matter—get the kind of nerve that lets them do what those two did that morning, right on through those attacks. Even when the rush was at its worse and bullets flying the thickest, those two stayed inside that brush shelter while the doctor worked at tending a sick and now wounded Indian boy. That pile of scanty brush over and around them would have done nothing to stop nor likely even deflect a bullet, yet neither of them made the first move toward safety. At least I could keep myself busy trying to do something about it all. They never even seemed to notice we were still under fire.

Sometime after the third attack Randolph crawled out into the sunlight. He stretched and then arched backward with his hands pressing at the small of his back. Well, I wouldn't wonder that his back should hurt after being cramped under that shelter so long.

"Is the kid all right?"

Randolph beamed. "By the grace of God and my own limited skills, I believe he will be. How is it out here, my boy?"

I shrugged. "I sure wish I knew. They could come again, or they might be a couple miles away right now. I just don't have any way of knowing what comes next. If anything."

"I've been thinking, lad. I have no knowledge of aboriginals, but I have heard that they make utterly inhuman efforts to recover their dead or their wounded." He smiled. "As a physician that comment captured my attention, you see."

"Yes, but what. . .?"

"Oh yes. The point of this. Of course. What I surmised was that the remaining warriors might be attempting to recover the bodies of those slain earlier, you see. Might I suggest that the next time we allow them to approach unmolested to carry away those bodies."

"Doctor, you have got more guts than I do," I admitted. "But I don't think I could stand here and watch them ride in that close without offering some defense."

"Then you do not believe my theory is sound?"

"Hell, doctor, you could have it figured right on the button for all I'd know. But if you turned out to be wrong it'd be awful tough potatoes for every one of us. They'd be so close by the time we knew for sure that it would likely be too late to fight. I just don't see that we have much choice about it. As long as they keep coming, we keep shooting." I think Dr. Randolph was a bit disappointed to hear me say I would keep on shooting at people, but what else could I do? I didn't know very much about wild Indians—aboriginals if you prefer— but from what little I had heard these fellows must have been of some plains tribe instead of the Apaches we'd been warned to expect around here. Which only meant I could know even less of what we could expect in the future. I would have to believe just absolutely anything that might happen. Expect anything at all.

I did sit down, though, and try to do some serious thinking on the general subject of hostiles. The main thing I could come up with was that they could do a job of killing. There was another thing that kept tugging at my memory. Something about...

"Doctor, we have to get out of here."

He snorted. "Impossible."

"No sir. I mean it this time. If I remember right, these fellows are more apt to come on us at night than the native tribes from around here. And they're awful stirred up about us now. They're sure to want to put us under quick before the locals come around to kill both them and us. And, doctor, you and I just don't have any chance of fighting off one of their rushes in the middle of the night. They'd have us for sure."

"Come now, McMurty. How many times do I have to tell you that the child cannot be moved? Now, more than ever before, he must be allowed to rest quietly."

"Doctor, this time we aren't talking about the possibility of being killed by those Indians. This time we're talking about almost certainly being killed if we stay here. And that is a very weak 'almost' when I say it. I really believe, doctor, that if we stay here we won't live to see the sun come up again. You and that boy you are so worried about and Jessica and me, doctor. Every one of us. So, if the boy can't live through being moved this afternoon he won't be cut short by more than a few hours."

He shook his head but more as if he were perplexed than really disbelieving. Maybe I was getting somewhere with him, anyway. For the sake of all of us I surely hoped so.

Randolph looked at the empty country around us, blinking his eyes and looking somehow out of place here in a way he never had before. I think it was just about that time right there that I came to believe that Dr. Randolph was truly a gentle man, in a way that I could never have understood before..

The doctor walked heavily, slump shouldered, to the wagon and found his pipe in the dashboard case there. He loaded it with great care and concentration and squandered a lucifer to light it, which was a habit of his when there was no fire handy to supply a coal. Using a match just to start a smoke always sort of got to me, but then I guess it might not have seemed so much to a city man like the doctor. And in truth I suppose it should not have been such a big thing to me either, for by now you could buy blocks or even boxes of cut matches nearly anywhere you might go. My reluctance to use one without good cause was nothing more than a hold-over habit from the bad times when I was a kid, during and just after the war.

Anyway, Randolph crawled up to the driving box of the wagon to sit and do his thinking. I left him to it and went to bring the horses in. I had been keeping an eye on them right along, but the Indians had not made any special effort to reach them. I guess they'd been thinking there would be plenty of time for that after we were dead and scalped.

Randolph had not said anything yet but at least he wasn't arguing. I went ahead and harnessed and hitched his team, then threw the gear onto the roan.

"All set, doctor," I said when I was done.

He sighed aloud, a long, heartsick sort of sound, and I wondered what it was costing him to agree to move the boy. I do not believe I could have dragged him away with the help of his team of grays had it not been for Jessica being there with us. Well, I might have been willing to gamble more myself if it hadn't been for her, and she was certainly special in her uncle's eyes. He made the only decision he could. "Very well," he said.

He climbed down from the wagon box and went to the shelter a few paces away. "You heard, Jessica?"

"Yes."

"You will sit with him in the wagon to comfort him, I hope."

"Of course."

"Then I suppose we must get on with it. Mr. McMurty?" He pointed to the boy lying in the shelter, and I stepped forward.

It took but a moment to strip the wagon side curtains and pull the brush apart. The boy was smaller than I remembered and much more pale. He did not look healthy, for a fact, and I did not wonder that the doctor would fear for him. I'm no expert but I would not have expected to see him breathe come the next morning whether we moved him now or not. He looked that bad.

I took his upper body and Randolph his legs and with Jessica hovering nearby like an oversized hummingbird we carried him gently to the bed in the wagon. He didn't weigh hardly a thing. I guess it was ungenerous of me, but every step of the way I was worrying not about maybe jostling the kid but about my rifle lying on the ground where the shelter had been. It would've been a really bad time for those Indians to show again.

I hurried back to retrieve my rifle while Jessica fussed and comforted beside the boy and Randolph stood nearby, looking solemn. I brought back the stack of side curtains and tossed them into the back of the wagon. We could take the time to replace them properly when the moment seemed somewhat better than this one. The only other things worth taking with us were a couple sacks, a crudely hammered knife and the water bag—all the possessions the boy had owned. "We are ready, Mr. McMurty," Randolph said.

"Yes sir. I'll tie my horse to the wagon, if you don't mind, and ride with you in the box."

"You have never done that before," the doctor said, puzzled.

"We weren't so sure of being hit by Indians then," I told him. "Now, well, if we get into a running fight they could hit my horse, and you'd be alone. This way we won't be separated regardless of what else happens."

He nodded. "Tie him and get in then. I want to get this over with as quickly as possible. No need for the child to suffer more than is necessary."

I looked into the back of the wagon. The boy did not seem to be suffering now. I was sure he could feel nothing, and that was undoubtedly a mercy. Better to be passed out than to feel the jolts ahead, for this road was a decent enough track by normal standards but was far from being smooth.

I had not given much thought to the boy. Randolph and Jessica had taken charge of his care, leaving me to concern myself with other matters. Now when I looked at him I wondered about him. Who and what he was. How he had come to be here alone with his sheep—scattered now and gone beyond recovery. How old he was. Whether he had a chance for life.

He really did look small lying there. And pale. I had never thought before of Indians being pale, but this boy was. His flesh was darker than mine but beneath that difference lay a pallor of ill health. His eyes were sunken now, set deep into the recesses of the sockets in a way that did not look natural. His mouth, the lips slightly parted over strong teeth, was rimmed with a nearly white ring of strain. Only his hair, thick and black and vibrantly alive with natural oils, looked healthy. Red stained bandages were wrapped around both of his thighs. A bullet must have passed through both legs.

I tied the roan to the back of the wagon and climbed inside onto the tangled nest of the side curtains. The doctor's vehicle was no longer so tidy as it had been. "All right, doctor. Any time you're ready."

I looked forward along the short length of the wagon. Jessica was seated on the floor of the bed, legs curled under her, one arm resting on the padded bench with the boy's head nestled in the crook of her arm. She was wedged between rows of boxes that lined the thin walls of the wagon box. They would give her some protection if the Indians came again, though I suspect she had chosen to sit there so she could be closest to the boy rather than for her own protection. Still, I could not have chosen a better spot for her.

Randolph, on the exposed driving seat, and the unconscious boy, lying on the bunk above the level of the wooden boxes, were much more vulnerable to fire. I could not think of a better place to put either of them, though, and did not want to speak aloud about places of relative safety within the wagon. I was afraid the girl might then want to put the boy on the floor and give up her protection for him.

As for myself, I wanted to be there in the back end of the box, so I could use the rifle to both sides and to the rear if need be.

Randolph picked up his driving lines and the grays jerked us forward into a walk and then, at his urging, into an unaccustomed fast trot. The roan followed obediently without setting back against the tied reins. Behind us I could hear the bleating of a few remaining sheep.

CHAPTER 22

I WAS SURPRISED THAT RANDOLPH HELD TO THE FAST ROAD gait he set for the grays, but he did it and they flat covered some miles that afternoon. I had no hope we could outrun the war party, but I sure did hope we could reach a town or some white men before they hit us again. And if it was their dead they wanted, they were welcome to them now.

What we had to settle for that evening was a shallow niche in the wall of yet another towering bluff, with which this country seemed to be liberally supplied. The opening was quite narrow, barely wide enough to admit the wagon. It was just what we needed—well, other than a town or a squadron of Yankee cavalry—since one man could easily defend it and there was no possibility of them coming at us in another of those mounted rushes. About all they could do that way would be to set themselves and their horses up as targets. Under the circumstances this place would do nicely.

Randolph unhitched his team, pulled the harness

from them and tied them to the wagon. I surely was glad to see that. I'd been afraid I would have trouble convincing him the animals would have to make do with the little grain and water we had left. There was no grass or browse of any kind in this little pocket, but now was not the time to be worried about the condition of the horses. Keeping them whole, and in our hands, was a lot more important.

When he was done tending his grays—and my roan equally well—the doctor climbed back into the wagon to take over care of the boy. Jessica got busy putting a meal together. As for what I'd been doing this whole while, I was taking it easy, seated comfortably at the entrance to our niche with the rifle across my knees.

The sounds behind me were pleasant ones, the girl rattling pots and the horses chewing. If it hadn't been for that threat of the Indians somewhere out in the descending darkness I would have been really comfortable here. After a while I heard light footsteps behind me.

"Did you want to eat with us at the wagon?" Jessica asked in that soft, ladylike voice of hers.

"Better not. I hope you don't mind."

"No. I thought you would want to eat here."

She bent beside me, and I could smell the rich odors of a flour thickened stew she had in a bowl. And, fainter, the clean girl-scent of her. I wonder if she somehow knew what I was thinking just then, for she asked, "Where do you come from, Mr. McMurty? Do you have a girl back home waiting for you?"

She sat and listened while I ate and between mouthfuls told her about Evelyn and the plans I had for locating my own piece of open range. I guess I got sort of carried away with it, telling her more than she probably would ever want to know about just the kind of grass and water I would be looking for and a motte or woodlot for the building of a house and to fuel it later and even the type of horses I would want to run, something like the roan with more weight and bone than the general run of half tamed mustangs you would expect to find on such an operation.

Telling her about it was good, though, and I was glad she was patient enough to wait through it all although she had not yet had her own meal. Telling her got me all caught up in my plans once again. For a while there they seemed to have slipped into the background.

"You really aren't a gunfighter then," she said when I finally shut up.

"No. I tried to tell you that once before."

"I'm sorry. I guess you did. Well . . . can I get you some coffee now?"

"I'd like that. Thanks."

She rose with easy grace. She was back in a moment with a steaming cup. "I'll bring you a refill after I've fed Uncle George." She sighed. "I imagine he will want to eat in the wagon, so he can be close to his patient."

It was fully dark now, and the moon would not be up for some time. I tried to keep my mind on the night sounds out toward the road.

"Back them out now, doctor. All clear out here." Randolph chirped to them and gave the lines a series of short tugs. The grays bowed their necks and pushed the wagon backward in a straight, controlled direction.

It was a clear and lovely morning, cool but not at all uncomfortable. You wouldn't think on a day this pretty that there could be trouble anywhere in the world. Jessica and Dr. Randolph seemed to feel the same. The only one who didn't get a lift out of the morning was the boy. He was still alive but seemed no improved from the day before.

I tied the roan to the wagon again and climbed into the back. Randolph clucked the team forward. He put them into a fast trot again. We couldn't be too far from the town now. We almost had to reach it before dark, possibly before noon if Randolph would hold to his pace. Maybe my worrying and the long, long night had been for nothing. Maybe those warriors had picked up their dead and gone.

The girl looked drawn, exhausted. Her eyes were puffy and dark rimmed. She had been up much of the night fretting over the boy while Randolph tried to help me keep watch at the entrance to the cut. None of us had gotten much sleep.

The road was considerably flatter here, winding back and forth among tall, carved projections of rock that were like nothing I had ever seen before. Or wanted to see again. If anything, there was less grass here than any place I had yet seen.

We jangled and rattled past yet another of the red-gray projections. Randolph's team gave a sharp, unexpected lurch forward, throwing me and the girl both off balance. Out of the corner of my eye I saw the roan, taken by surprise as we were, jerked by his reins. The leather snapped, and he was running free behind us but following.

The grays had picked it up into a hard run. The wagon was leaping about in the road bed like a pitching bronc, and choking dust was swirling through the open body. For one instant as I clutched at the sideboards trying to brace myself I thought Dr. Randolph had lost his mind. Then I heard the shots and the too familiar whoops and yells of the red men. Well, that sure answered that question. They hadn't been willing to collect their dead and quit there.

This time, though, things were much different than before. This time the Indians were on foot, with solid positions to shoot from. This time we were bouncing and flopping so that I couldn't begin to draw a fine bead on anything, what little of the scrap I could see through all the dust.

I began to work the lever and throw shots through the open sides of the wagon in the blind hope that maybe they would do some good. No wonder I had thought the Indians were such rotten shots. Hell, I'd have been lucky to hit a cliff face fifty yards away with all the bumping and thrashing going on. I think I was in the air more than I was touching wood.

I took a look forward in the wagon—it could not have made much difference whether I kept shooting or not—and saw the girl trying to hang onto the sideboards with one hand and to steady the kid with the other.

"Lie down, dammit. In the bed of the wagon," I shouted at her. I don't know why I screamed it so loud. She wasn't more than a half-dozen feet away, and except for the crackle of gunfire coming now from behind us there was not much noise. I guess it just seemed like it should have been noisy. A nonexistent din of battle or something.

Jessica gave me a grim and frightened look, but she said nothing. Neither did she do what I told her. She kept hanging onto that Indian boy, trying to help him.

I went back to my noise-making with the Winchester. I kept it up until the magazine ran dry, then sat and watched and waited. If they got to their ponies and came after us there was not really all that much I could hope to do about it.

They quit firing too as the gap between us widened beyond a quarter mile. The whole thing had taken no more than a fistful of seconds, a few dozen ticks on a Horologe. I reloaded the rifle. I could see no pursuit coming at us through the trailing dust, thank goodness. And the roan was running strong beside the wagon. He seemed all right.

When they were a mile behind I hollered forward over my shoulder, "I think you can slow them down now, doctor." For a moment there was no answer.

I heard a choking moan. I turned to look. The first thing I saw was the girl. She had a look of slack-jawed horror. Beyond her the doctor was crumpled in the driving box. The stout grays continued their panicked dash.

I let the rifle fall to the bed of the wagon and crawled forward, having to hold onto the sides to keep from being thrown down by the swaying and thumping of the wagon. Jessica kept staring at her uncle.

I had to crawl over Jessica and the Indian boy to get to the driving box. The pounding motion of the wagon threw me off balance, what little I had, and my knee rammed cruelly into the boy's ribs. He never flinched, though.

The grays were still running hard, lathering heavily now from the burden of the fat they carried. I dove through the opening between the bed and the driving box. I ended up sprawled across the seat and on Dr. Randolph, but I got hold of the lines and hauled back on them. "Easy, girls. Whoa, babies. That's it, girls. Bring it down now."

They tucked their heads to the bits but kept on pounding. "Whoa, dammit!" I released the pressure and then snatched at their mouths, hard. They began to give to it.

I managed to get out onto the seat and brace against the dashboard. The grays came down to a trot. "Jessica. Get my rifle and come up here."

She said nothing, but I heard her scrambling around back there. In a moment she joined me on the seat.

"I'm going to stop them now," I told her. "I'll have to be paying attention behind us. Just in case. I... I'm sorry, but I'll have to ask you to see if there is anything that can be done for your uncle. I hope you understand." She nodded. She looked awfully pale.

The grays came gratefully to a halt, stiff-legged and blowing. I jumped from the wagon and hurried around behind it. There was no sign of anyone behind us.

The roan had stopped nearby. He was not breathing nearly so hard as the grays. He let me walk to his head and take hold of his bit. I led him to the wagon and tied the broken reins to the bit rings. It was better than nothing. Still no sign of pursuit. Maybe this time they figured us even.

I eased back toward the front of the wagon. Jessica was sitting bolt upright on the driving seat. Tear tracks streaked her face. She looked at me, her eyes bleak.

"Uncle George is dead," she said dully. "The little boy died too. Both of them."

She looked empty. Totally empty. That was the only way to put it. I had really been some big help to these people. Yeah, I'd really given them a lot of the protection they needed. It was a good thing I had never claimed to be a gunfighter for I surely had failed them in that regard. But what else could I have done? I didn't know. There must have been something.

I helped the girl out of the wagon and sat her in the shade while I tugged and shoved Dr. Randolph's body into the back of the wagon and straightened him out there. She acted like a sleepwalker when I helped her back into the wagon.

We reached the next town inside of an hour. We'd been that damned close.

CHAPTER 23

"Miss Randolph, I don't know what to say. I wish there was something... anything more than I could do."

She shook her head. "There is nothing. Really. Nor anything more you could have done before. Please don't blame yourself, Mr. McMurty. I certainly don't place any blame on you."

"Yes, well..." What else could I say? Dr. Randolph was dead. There was sure nothing I could do now to change that. "What about you now, Jessica? Will you be all right?"

She shrugged, then almost smiled. "I'll be all right. I'll take nurse's training more than likely. He would have approved of that."

The girl was seated in the light rockaway that operated as a stage down to Tucson where she could make connection with the Overland route through to El Paso and then back East. Within a couple weeks she would be home. Maybe she could forget about it then. She had been pretty shaken up by the experience, which was only to be expected. It had been rough on her.

We'd been here three days now and she seemed somewhat less keyed up than she had been. I had helped with what I could, arranging for Dr. Randolph's burial—and the boy as well, at her insistence, though they would not allow the boy in the regular cemetery plot—and selling the team and wagon and such things as that. The doctor's records and the stuff he had collected on his trip were being freighted back East.

"I'll be all right, Mr. McMurty. Honestly." She adjusted her bonnet and sat stiffly on the hard seat. She seemed to have herself under tight control, but I guess she was all right. I got the idea she wanted this whole thing put behind her and maybe would prefer that I go.

"Well, if there's nothing more..."

"No. Thank you. But there isn't a thing."

"Yes, ma'am. Well, take care now." She looked my way and gave me a polite, insincere smile. "Good-bye, Jessica."

"Good-bye, Mr. McMurty."

I turned and left her there without waiting for the rig to leave, which might not have been the proper and polite thing to do but seemed best under the circumstances. I glanced back a few times, but she was not looking in my direction.

I started toward the nearest saloon—I hadn't wanted to be checking in any of them while I still had Jessica Randolph to watch after—but halfway there changed my mind and veered instead toward a small eatery beside it.

The counter man brought me coffee that was hot and fresh and good, and I sipped at it slowly.

For some reason I felt a nagging, uneasy reluctance to go on looking for Bud Terry and Little Jimmy Childress. I don't know why that should have been, for nothing had changed. I still owed that money to my neighbors, and there was still a good chance Terry and his friend would yet have some of it. But I kept thinking of Dr. Randolph and the waste of all that ability to help people when he died. He had spent his life learning how to heal. Here I was, going around killing people. And looking for two more fellows that I might—probably would—have to draw on. I fingered the butt of the big Dragoon. I hoped I wouldn't have to use it again.

I drained off the rest of the coffee and forced aside the lethargy that kept trying to glue my tail to the stool. I paid the counter man and left. There was a strong temptation to throw my gear onto the roan and see just how fast he could get me back to Texas and home. If it had been just my own money at stake I think I would have turned toward the livery. Instead I walked next door to that saloon.

The barkeep there looked enough like the restaurant counter man to be his brother and come to think of it with the two places side by side it was very possible that they were brothers. Both of them looked like they would be at home on a horse more than behind a counter. Trim, competent looking fellows who did not volunteer unwelcome gab at their customers.

I ordered a beer and nibbled at a bowl of popped corn on the bar top while I listened to the conversations around me. The place was not real busy nor too noisy, about eight or ten others standing on the buying side of the bar. They were a mixed bag of mining and town type people, and their talk rambled over subjects like the stock market and loose women and the territorial government and other such things of little interest to my ears.

The barkeep paused to draw me a refill and place a fresh bowl of the salted popped corn before me, and I put my question to him. Had he seen anything of Terry or Childress, or might he know where I could reach them? He looked at me with some curiosity.

"You're the fellow that had a scrap with some Indians a few days ago, aren't you?" I admitted that I was. "I would've thought that would be enough for one man for a while," he said.

"I'm not looking for trouble with anyone," I told him. "I just need to find these fellows to set something right. Though I have heard they are a rough pair at times."

"There's no 'at times' about it. If ever a human person was purely worthless it would be that Childress. I don't know Terry, but I've heard the same could be said of him."

"You know Childress then?"

"The whole town does, and I can tell you this. You won't find him or any of his crowd anywhere around here." He was sort of grinning when he said that.

"Don't stop there," I urged.

"If you insist," he said agreeably. "Matter of fact, we're sorta proud of what happened. It was about, oh, six months ago that it happened. Childress and a bunch of those yahoos that run with him braced a scared little drummer in town here. A little dry goods salesman from back East, he was, but friendly and never a bother to anyone.

"Anyway, I don't know what that bunch of hardcases

wanted of him, but they were fixing to devil him and were waving guns and knives in the air and generally raising hell so the poor little fellow was white and shaking like an aspen leaf in a stiff breeze. One of Childress' bunch, name of Randy something-or-other, decided to cut the little fellow's vest buttons off for a souvenir or something. He did a poor job of it and drew some blood on the guy's wrist. Damned if the little drummer didn't dip into his pocket and come out with one of those wee bitty .22 rimfire revolvers like the ladies sometimes carry in their muffs. Planted one of those tiny bullets smack into that yahoo's heart and dropped him like a slaughtered hog, prob'ly as much from surprise as from the bullet.

"Next thing those hardcases could think of was to hang the little fellow, and him blubbering and carrying on because he'd killed a man. Though, of course, that Randy had it coming to him for cutting on the drummer.

"Well sir, the other boys around at the time— geologists and shopkeepers and the town barber and a bunch more who like to see fair play—they stepped in and put a stop to that and sent the drummer safely out of town on the next coach, which was just then loading, thank goodness.

"Now don't you know that Childress and his boys got to sulking about that and wouldn't learn the easy way. A few days later they came back into town and holed up with a bunch of whiskey, saying they were going to take over the whole town to use as a headquarters, and all of us could just leave or they'd shoot up the town and all of us still in it." He chuckled a little.

"We didn't take all that kindly to the notion and,

Lordy, I'll bet most of the men here have fought either Indians or Yankees or Rebels or a combination from among those. There isn't hardly anyone who can't handle himself in a shooting fight. So, the bluff didn't work too good. Next thing Childress and his boys knew, they'd been herded together, stripped of every weapon they carried and turned loose with not a hat nor a boot among them. They haven't offered to come back since."

No wonder he'd been grinning. "Sounds like you did get your lesson across," I told him, "and the more power to you. If everyone would stand up to those rannies and the others like them, I'll bet that breed would die out in no time."

"Could be," he said. "It's for sure no one in this town will take water from any of the rough ones again. We by damn don't have to. We proved that right enough."

"You sure enough did," I told him, "but in the meantime I still have to look those fellows up for a bit of talk. Any idea where I might find them?" The man rubbed at the back of his neck. He seemed to be pondering. I heard the rattle of traces and a shout from outside. The stage seemed to be just now pulling out. Jessica Randolph was on her way home now. Nothing more I could do for her or for her uncle. And I did have other things to worry about anyway.

"I notice you didn't say just what it was you wanted with them," the fellow said.

"No sir. You could say it is a personal matter." Another man at the bar, a beefy fellow who'd been drinking hard liquor and maybe too much of it for this or any other time of day, moved closer to us and dipped a fat hand into the bowl of popped com the barkeep had set in front of me. "Hell, Bernie," the drinking man said. "Look at 'im. Big ol' gun on 'is belly. Mean look in 'is eyes. Aw, you've heard of 'im. This's the kid goin' around gunnin' ever'-body from that crowd." The idiot sort of leered my way— more of a smirk really— and added, "They say he's killed five of 'em so far."

I felt myself go cold inside. For one brief flicker of time I felt a terrible urge to shut him up. With that Dragoon. I stiffened. Very, very carefully I laid both hands onto the bar. Speaking slowly and as deliberately as I could manage, I told the barkeeper, "Your friend has his facts wrong, mister. I would appreciate it if someone else would do the correcting of him."

The barkeeper had been giving me an intent look, as much curiosity as anything else as far as I could tell. He turned to another man standing a little further down the bar. "Stan, lead him off to a cup of coffee or something, would you?"

"Sure." The customer poured a glass of whiskey for bait, took my surly, burly friend by the arm and led him out the front door.

"Now, mister," the barkeep said, turning back to me, "you said there were some facts wrong there. Care to tell me what the truth is?"

"Just to tell you that I'm no gunfighter. And I'm not setting out looking to kill any man. Not Childress. Not Terry. And certainly not any honest citizen, which I understand would leave those fellows out. In any case, I don't want to go after anyone. They just have something that belongs to some friends of mine, and I'm responsible for getting it back."

"Uh huh." He seemed to be doing some thinking again. He drifted down the bar to do some refill work and came back to me. "What I've heard lately," he said, "and we do try to keep up with such things, is that Childress and his boys have been hanging out around Fort Sumner of late."

"That's over in New Mexico Territory, isn't it?"

"Uh huh. South and east of Santa Fe it is."

"Well, I guess I'll thank you for the help then and be on my way," I told him. I drained off the last of my beer and laid a dime on the bar.

He picked up the dime and slid it into a pocket of his apron. "There's a wagon road to the east," he said. "It joins the north-south road a couple miles north of here. You can't hardly miss it, but right there where it joins it looks like a spur off to the south. It's the right way, though. Take it, and you'll find what you're looking for."

I thanked him again and left, heading for the livery where the roan was being tended. I was walking warily now, though. There was something in the air here that I couldn't pin down but that made me uneasy nonetheless. I paid off what I owed on the roan and got out of there without laying over until morning like I normally might have done.

CHAPTER 24

I CAME TO THE JUNCTION JUST BEFORE DARK AND LIKE THE barkeeper had said, it sure looked like another south-leading fork into some rough country. It was a narrow, twisting track that I could not see along for more than a quarter mile or so. No doubt it curved east somewhere not far south of the Y.

It being already so late I decided to stop where I was for the night. I pulled my sack from the roan and hobbled him but did not try to picket him. He'd been grained for the past three days but there was no point in tying him away from the little bit of feed he might be able to find here. The growth was certainly not what you'd call lush, not anywhere around here that I had seen.

I was not really very hungry and was still feeling a little spooked about the thought of roaming Indians, so I decided to make do without a fire. I made my supper from a handful of crackers and some cold boiled beef that I'd picked up in town, spread my blankets out of sight from the road and curled up for an early sleep.

As early as I wakened the next morning someone else was up earlier yet, for as I was sitting in my blankets trying to decide if I should boil a can of coffee just for myself I heard a rattle of harness on the roadway. I pulled on my hat and boots and went to see who or what it might be at such an hour.

A light freight wagon was rumbling down from the north, drawn by a four-horse hitch of poorly bred but willing enough animals. They were plopping their big hooves along at a steady job. I stepped out from behind the rocks where I'd been sleeping and waved to the driver of the noisy rig.

The poor fellow like to have had a heart attack when I stepped out so unexpectedly. He'd been sitting slumped and comfortable on his bench, but when he spotted me he jerked upright. He let out a groan I could hear even across the distance between us. He hauled his team to a stop and shoved his hands into the air. "I ain't armed," he yelled.

I went over to him, shaking my head. "Man, oh man," I told him when I was close enough. "I guess I know now how bad I look without a morning shave. But all I was doing when I walked out here was looking for someone to have coffee with this morning."

He was an older man with a shaggy, mostly white beard and straggling hair and yellowing teeth. He dropped his arms down and took up his driving lines again. At first, he looked like he was going to get mad. Then he grinned and laughed at himself.

"Sure takes a lot of turnin' around in a man's thinking, that does. I thought sure you was a road agent of some sort. Sure did." He chuckled. "Scairt me outta ten years, boy, an' I cain't hardly afford that." He snorted and spat a brown stream behind the hocks of his near wheeler. "Well hell, boy, if that offer's still open I reckon I'll join ye. Give me a chance to unwind from my fright, if ya know what I mean."

"Good enough," I told him. "Get your team settled, and I'll get the coffee to going."

I had the fire started and a can of water set over it by the time he joined me. He squatted and watched while I poured a handful of ready-ground beans into the water. I gave him my name and he told me his. Everett Goble, he said he was.

"You get an early start, Mr. Goble," I told him. It was yet barely light enough to see, and his team had worked up a good sheen of sweat already.

"A man doesn't seem to need so much sleep when he gets to be my age, boy," he said, "an' if I'm gonna be awake I might's well be doing something with myself."

"Yes sir," I said, trying to be polite to the old boy. "I didn't notice any freight company signs on your rig." I observed, so as to have something to say. "Most outfits like to show their names."

He cackled and spat. "That's right, boy. No comp'ny letters on my rig. Not on your life, boy. No sirree-Bob. Everett Goble works for himself an' no other. Always has an' always will."

"You are in the freighting business, though, I take it?"

"I am," he said and gave me a little hint of a bow with his upper body that made him reach fast to catch himself from falling as he was still squatting and hadn't sat.

"Oops!" He bowed again, his dignity unruffled by anything so minor as that small loss of balance.

"You see, boy," he said, "I am kinda independent minded. I go wherever the winds or a load o' freight takes me. Ever'where you go, somebody always has somethin' that needs carryin' to someplace else. Me an' my four boys there always has work to do, an' it's carried us all acrost an' up and down this country."

He chuckled again. "Started out from Alabama more'n thirty year ago. Been to Californy four times, as far north as Quebec an' as far south as Mexico City, and I still enjoy every turn of the wheel. A man couldn't ask for more'n I got."

"Your four boys?" I asked, wondering when they might be along.

"Yes. You seen 'em. My geldings." He grinned. "My family changes members from time to time, but they're all my boys, sure enough they are. They do right by me, an' I do right by them. When one of 'em gets the gray around his muzzle I find a good home for 'im an' pay someone to pasture and tend 'em for as long as they live. It's the least I can do, I figure. An' in case you ain't noticed, which you ain't, your coffee is boilin'."

I reached quick to pull the can aside and from my canteen sloshed in a little cold water on the theory that would settle the grounds, which it sometimes seems to help do though I don't believe I've ever once drunk boiled coffee without chewing some grounds while I was doing it.

"It's too bad folks don't do the same for people when they get old and ailing," I said.

Now the way this old boy had already been so quick to talk about age, his own and his horses', I was expecting some sort of long-drawn lament from him when I opened that particular door. But not from Everett Goble did I get one.

He cackled and grinned some more while I poured the coffee and took a first, steaming sip before he spoke. "Now I don't worry about such as that, boy," he told me. "You see, I figure to keep myself in harness 'til the day I drop. An' after that I got it all worked out, see. Got it set down on paper just what I want done." He patted a pocket on his sweat-stained shirt, and his grin got all the bigger.

"Had me a will drawn up by a drunken lawyer one day, but it's all writ down an' proper now, it is. An' it's likely to drive some judge certified loco when the time comes to use it. You see," he said with a wink, "when I croak they're to have me tended special."

"I wanta be skinned, you see, an' tanned into soft leather. An' made up into one o' them sidesaddle rigs like the classy women ride. Then for the rest o' time, boy, I'll be between the two things I love the best." He nodded firmly. "Yes sir. A good horse an' a pretty woman."

He clapped his hands in delight with himself, and I laughed right along with him.

"Mr. Goble, you are like no one else I've ever met."

"Hell, boy, I ain't ashamed of being one of a kind. An' you make pretty decent coffee for bein' no more than a pup."

"Thank you kindly."

I dragged out more hard crackers and the last of my

boiled beef—which would spoil soon anyway if it wasn't eaten—and we munched while we finished the coffee.

"Now that wasn't half bad, boy," he said when we were done. "I'm in your debt for sure." "My pleasure, Mr. Goble. I'm glad for your company. Wasn't expecting it."

"Umph," he grunted. He seemed pleased though. He sighed and shifted but did not rise. I took the hint.

"What do you think, Mr. Goble? Should we boil those grounds one more time?"

He came nimbly to his feet, not at all reluctant to move now. "My turn to supply the water," he said cheerfully. He disappeared behind the rocks and was back a moment later with a well filled water bag. "Just filled it this morning. Good and fresh."

It was, too, and we had a can of it heating a moment later. The old man settled happily by the fire and threw a few stray sticks into it. Well, I hadn't been lying to him. I was glad for his company. He was a genuinely likeable fellow.

"Would it be too personal for me to ask where you're bound, boy?"

"Why, I don't mind at all, Mr. Goble. I'm heading for New Mexico. Fort Sumner actually."

His face fell. "Aw, now. I was kinda hoping you was going south. I would've enjoyed you riding along." He shrugged. "In the meantime, though, I'll jus' be enjoyin' your coffee. An' havin' someone to talk to. Other than my boys, that is. They're good comp'ny too most of the time."

The water reached a fast boil. This time Mr. Goble felt free enough to pull the can to the side and pour the cool water in himself.

"There," he said. "Let that steep a minit an' it'll be as good as your mama could make for you, boy." He rubbed his hands. "Nothin' better than a cup of coffee of a mornin', specially when you have fresh water to make it with. Yes sirree-Bob.

"Say now," he went on. "If you're headed New Mexico way you'll pass a real good spring inside of five miles. Off the road, though. You can't see it without you know where to look."

I nodded. "I'd be indebted if you'd give me the directions then," I told him, which seemed to please him. That was why I'd said it, really. If I couldn't spot his wagon tracks leaving the public road there was something wrong with me.

"What you do, then, is to straight on north for, oh, call it just under five miles, boy. You'll come to a big red rock on the west side with a... what's wrong?" He stopped short.

I guess I did have an odd sort of expression hanging out for the world to see. "You said to go on north five miles? Isn't this the turn-off right here to carry me east?"

"East? Hell no, boy. This turn jus' goes south for seven, eight miles to a little ole knot of Mex'can adobes an' a tradin' post where the Navaho come in to swap their wool an' stuff. There's sure no road down there leadin' east, and I oughta know. I've traveled it a couple times hauling stuff for J.T. Biggerstaff that runs the place." He shook his head. "Sure, am glad I ran into you, boy. You'd have wasted half the day takin' that turn."

"Yeah," I said. "At least that much."

At least that much and probably a whole lot more. A

whole lot more. That barkeeper named Bernie had been awfully specific about which turn I was to take. Just as he'd been real specific about letting me know he was no friend of Little Jimmy Childress.

Well, after what that drinking man had said I knew good and well they had heard of a man of my description on the shoot for Childress and Terry. That made it real interesting.

It seemed pretty simple. Send me off to the north and then back south again. They—he— could drop a word to the right someone, maybe pick up a few dollars for his trouble. And that right someone and maybe some friends could cut across country and be there waiting by the time I would pass along that road to nowhere. Yeah, it made sense.

Mr. Goble would never know just how much I was indebted to him. He went on talking, pleased with himself, and finished giving me the directions to that spring of good, fresh water. I listened, but my mind was not much on what he was saying.

CHAPTER 25

THE NARROW TRACK OF LITTLE-TRAVELED ROADWAY WAS OFF to my left. Here, on higher ground, the going was rough but nothing that any decent horse would find hard to handle. The roan picked his way ahead at a fast walk without making a fuss about it.

The Y of the main road was a couple miles to the north. Mr. Goble had hitched up and gone rumbling south toward town still glad he had saved me the inconvenience of making a wrong turn.

Well, he had saved me an awful lot maybe, but not that. I was surely going to take that road now, but a whole lot better prepared than I would have been. That was why I avoided the road itself but was riding parallel to it, back where I should not be readily seen by whoever was waiting up ahead.

The roan was quite willing to take a faster pace even over this uncertain footing, but I kept him down to the walk. I wanted no dust raised that might draw attention my way.

The sun kept climbing and several more miles passed behind, and I began to wonder if I might have been mistaken if that barkeeper might have made an honest mistake. From what Goble had said I should be better than half way down to the trading post community by now.

Off to the east the empty road curved out of sight behind a sharp knob. Beyond that knob I could see where the track continued southward. I might have ridden right on past except for a flicker of sunlight reflecting off something on the near side of the knob.

I reined the roan to a stop with some brush between me and whatever might be over there. From a distance just under a half mile I could not see anything now. The reflection was not repeated.

I decided caution would do a whole lot more for me than laziness, so I pulled the rifle from its boot and stepped off the horse. I gave the reins a wrap around some greasewood and left the roan tied there. This might not be a good time for pulling the bridle and putting on hobbles. I might be coming back in a big hurry. And if it happened that I did not come back at all, the horse could break his reins if he got thirsty enough. That would likely take several days, as solid and well trained as he seemed to be. Why, I would almost trust this one to stand ground reined for more than a few minutes. There was no really good cover between me and the knob. No washes or gullies such as would have been so welcome. Still, there were a few clumps of straggly brush and prickly pear, and these I kept between me and the knob as best I could. I made sure there was a shell in the chamber of the rifle and walked ahead.

The ground was hard under my boots and gritty, but it made no great amount of noise except to my own ears, I'm sure. But it did sound awfully loud to me.

I felt terribly exposed on that flat, mostly bare ground. Thinking about that, wondering if someone might be lying in ambush ahead of me, I had a powerful yen to get down close to the ground and sneak ahead like a kid playing at settlers 'n Indians. About the only thing keeping me from doing it was thinking about how silly that would look—though to whom I could not have said.

I went closer, moving more slowly as I came near. I could see no one and nothing except the scrubby brush and the barren, lifeless dirt.

Behind a screen of gray-green brush I caught a hint of movement. I stared at the area but could see nothing. I looked away and brought my eyes back and this time— like suddenly finding one of those faces drawn into a picture of a tree so that after once seeing it you could not understand how you ever missed seeing it before—I could see the shape of a horse there. And beside it were others.

I crept closer. There were no men nearby, but four saddled horses were tied there. A coyote dun, two chest- nuts and a nearly black bay. One of them shifted the weight of its hindquarters from one foot to another. The movement caused a short flash of sunlight reflecting on a saddle concha. It must have been just such a chance reflection that had first caught my eye.

I eased up to the animals and looked them over

better. They were all in good flesh but were hard muscled, with no fat to slow them down. At the saddle of each was a rifle boot. And each of the four of these was empty.

Well, this was what I'd been expecting to find. This or something very much like it. I suppose I shouldn't have been surprised or upset to find it now, but the reality of knowing there were four men with rifles lying in wait for me was a whole lot different from the idea of thinking someone might be.

And in many ways, this was different from anything I had faced before. For the first time it was up to me to do some real hunting instead of waiting and reacting to what other people chose to do. At least this way maybe I could have some control over what happened for a change.

I skirted the patch of brush where the horses were tied and began to climb the rising slope of the knob. I was moving slower than ever now, placing my feet carefully so to make no noise and going up one step at a time. Whoever these people were, their attention would be on the road. From here they could see it for a long way to the north and would expect to have plenty of warning. And by now they should be getting plenty bored. They might be wandering around and looking in most any direction, simply for the lack of anything better to do with themselves while they waited for their target to blunder under their guns.

I inched upward to the top of the knob, rounded and totally bare. I had no thoughts now of what might look foolish. I rolled the hammer of the rifle back to full cock and got down on my belly. I crawled forward, terribly conscious of the grate of rock and dirt under me.

They were just on the far side of the knob, maybe fifteen feet lower than I was and sixty or seventy feet ahead. They were screened from the road by a string of nail cask-sized rocks. From the scruff marks on the ground it looked like at least some of those rocks had been put there for this occasion.

All four of them were there behind the rocks like so many mice in a nest, and I was almighty glad to see that. It would have been a lot touchier if one or two of them had been straying elsewhere when I got to them.

They were young fellows each one and dressed fancy in bright colored shirts and pretty boots and with hats that'd never been caked thick with the dust raised by a bunch of cattle. They were clean shaven, cheerful looking fellows close to my own age. For some reason they reminded me of Lee Miles.

Three of the four were leaning back against the rocks smoking and chattering. They looked relaxed and comfortable and not at all bored the way I would have expected. The fourth one was sitting on one of the rocks keeping an eye out toward the north. Their rifles—saddle carbines they were really, and shiny new every one— were leaned within easy reach. They all wore revolvers too, one of them dragging his belt down with a pair of holstered wheel-guns.

Seeing that reminded me of what I was doing here, and I quit making comparisons between these boys and Lee Miles. These nice-looking boys had come here with the idea of putting some bullets into me as a favor to Little Jimmy Childress. I was just sure of that.

It was a shame that neither Bud Terry nor Childress was here with them. I was really wanting to get this done with. I wanted to go home.

There was no point in putting this off now that I was where I needed to be. I raised up to my knees and brought the butt of the rifle to my shoulder.

"Easy does it now, boys," I called. "Stay right where you are."

My, but that did get their attention. They went absolutely rigid. The one sitting by himself on the rock looked like he was about to grab for his gun but none of them did.

"That's it, boys. Nice and still. Now. Were you fellas looking for me?"

Four heads were shaken back and forth. "We don't even know who you are, mister," one of them hollered.

"Boys, you can say it, but you can't make me believe it. What we're going to do is this. One at a time, starting from my left, you guys are going to lay your guns on the ground and step over to the side. Ten feet would do just fine," I told them. "Before we start, you might want to know where we stand, what happens if you try me. My sights will be on the one lifting iron. If any of the others moves, I'll pull the trigger on him before I go for the rest of you. And you may have heard I am a passable fair shot. Now let's go ahead and do this. You first, fella."

The one on the rock stood. With two fingers of his right hand he lifted his revolver free of the leather. He bent and laid it carefully on the ground before he moved to the side.

When he stopped I swung the muzzle of the rifle toward the chest of the next one in line. He stood and copied the actions of the first one.

The man with the brace of pistols was next. They looked like fancy things, the grips made of some light-colored material that stood out against the darker colors of his clothes. When he stood he worked his mouth as if he wanted to spit but he did not, nor did he say anything. Very, very gently he laid the two revolvers in the dirt and stepped away.

The last one rose, shrugged and dropped his gun to the ground. The idiot was lucky it didn't go off. If it had startled me I might have jerked the trigger by accident, and I doubt he would have approved of the result had that happened.

Me, I felt one whale of a lot better once all that hardware was on the ground and no longer such a temptation.

As soon as they were all disarmed and were together again I motioned them toward me. They shuffled reluctantly forward. When they were closer I took the rifle down from my shoulder and let it hang in my left hand. At this range the old Dragoon would be quicker and more accurate. I hoped they understood that.

"Boys," I told them, "we need to do a little talking. Which of you heads this pack?"

They stopped and looked at each other and after a minute or so the one who'd been on the rock took a half step closer. He hiked his chin up a bit and said, "I'll talk for us. What we got to say anyway, which won't be much."

"Uh huh. Well, we'll see about that in a minute. You see, I'm getting awful tired of having total strangers try to kill me. It tends to make me irritable, you see. So, when I ask you something it'd be a good idea for you to answer. Otherwise I may just cut you down and go on to the next fellow with my questions. Understood? Because I've got several of you to choose from and don't really need any one in particular, right?"

He swallowed hard and nodded. He must have been hearing some of those stories about a crazy gunman named McMurty going after the blood of the Childress crowd. I hoped he had. Anyway, he seemed plenty willing to believe what I told him.

"All right?"

He nodded again. He was starting to look a bit green, which was just what I wanted. I'd much rather scare the fool out of them than have to shoot anyone.

"Now. Who sent you here?"

"Bernie," he said quickly. "Bernie Marth. He told us you'd be on this road."

Well, that was just what I'd expected, what it pretty much had to be. "Why didn't Childress come himself? Or Bud Terry?"

The guy's chin came up a bit and he firmed his jaw. "He'd have been here. You can bet on that, mister. Jimmy ain't afraid of you nor any other man."

"Where is he then?"

I got nothing but silence in return. The man had a set, stubborn look on him.

"It's up to you," I said, deliberately mild about it. "I can always ask the next in line."

He just stared at me like a beef gone into a lull until one of the others murmured, "Go ahead an' tell him, Dipsy. Jimmy'd like nothing better than to get a look at this fella. It'd be doin' the boss a real favor."

It was a nice line of reasoning, and I wished I had thought of it myself.

The first man glanced around at his friend. He gave the other gunman a weak smile and seemed more than a little relieved to hear that way out. The other two nodded their agreement to him.

He turned back to me and shrugged. "Him and Terry and a couple others rode over to Fort Sumner. You might find 'em there if you got the guts to face them." He was feeling some better now. "But if you got any sense you'll run like hell, 'cause if Jimmy ever finds you you're a dead man for sure."

"I have to thank you for your advice, friend, but as I recall I'm not the one that's been doing the running lately. And now, just to show you that I don't have a thing against taking good advice when I hear it, I'll ask you boys to shuck out of your hats and boots and gun belts. And when you finally get back to town, you can tell your friend Bernie Marth all about it. He ought to get a big kick out of the whole thing since it was really his idea."

From the looks on their faces those boys would have preferred it if I'd shot them. But that barkeeper had had a real good idea when he was spinning that yarn for me. I didn't at all mind adopting the best parts of it.

I wondered briefly if I might have caused some future discomfort for Mr. Marth. Gee, I wouldn't want to do that, though. He had been such a helpful fellow.

When finally, I rode out of there I was leading four extra horses, and on the saddle of each was tied a gun belt, a fancy pair of boots and a clean, pretty hat. I figured I could dump the surplus gear and turn the horses loose a few miles down the road. Say, somewhere over in New Mexico Territory. In the meantime, those limping boys could keep themselves amused by cussing me while they walked. I guess I whistled some as I moved along.

CHAPTER 26

IT SURE WAS AN IMPROVEMENT TO BE BACK AT LEAST WITHIN a few miles of my home state, no matter the days and days of riding that still would have been needed to get home. If, that is, I was able to go home. I sure had some high hopes anyway, if only I could find Childress and Terry. And my neighbors' money.

I had avoided Santa Fe this time through although I'd had to pass right by it to get down to the eastern part of the territory. There was nothing I needed in that city, though, and there might have been trouble if I'd run into any of Childress' friends there. And I'd been a whole lot happier getting past those boys in Arizona without having to burn powder. I was having some big thoughts about maybe working the same kind of thing with Childress and Terry.

Fort Sumner turned out to be a bare and ugly collection of adobe buildings with more civilians living there than the handful of blue-shirts. Apparently it was an army buying point for beef and for horses. There were

enough sturdy pens on the flat near the place to handle
quite a few head of stock, anyway. One pen held fifty or
sixty scrub ponies. Another held about a hundred head
of such bony, slab-sided, long--legged, patch-coated
beeves that I got downright homesick just looking at
them. They were so ugly and mean looking they could
have been a bunch of cactus boomers caught out of the
brush country down below our place.

I rode over to the pens and sat for a time just enjoying
looking at them. It was good to see them, but I did have
one small disappointment. The blocky roan tipped his
ears in their direction when we came near but he did not
get all hotted up and light footed at the sight of the herd.
It was plain he had a head for a different kind of business
than mine was.

I scratched the horse on his poll and spun him away
from the beeves. We weren't here for cow work anyway,
and I surely could have no complaint with this animal.

There was a cantina at the edge of the place—I
couldn't quite decide if Fort Sumner was more town or
fort—and I stopped there. I sat on the horse for a
moment, unwilling right then to step down and go inside,
for once I did there might be no turning back.

It was almost certain that my description had been
spread around here. Childress and Terry might even be
inside themselves by some blind chance.

Finding them was what I wanted, of course. But
dammit I was tired of being on the shoot all the time.

I stepped off the roan and gave the reins a wrap
around a cedar pole someone had strapped across some

short posts. A number of other horses were already tied there.

The inside of the cantina was nearly dark in comparison with the bright sunlight outside, and I had a real bad moment when I first realized I couldn't see well enough to keep an eye on the people in there. It took several long, heart-thumping seconds for my eyes to adjust, more than enough time for someone to draw and shoot if I'd run into the wrong crowd there. That really shook me, for I should not have been so careless. I would not dare make another slip until this was over and done with.

I blinked and wiped my palms against my jeans. My hands had started to sweat.

The place was more crowded than I would have thought from the number of horses outside, but most of the customers were wearing uniforms. There seemed to be a lot of them off duty, and I wondered if this was normal or if it might be a Sunday. I had lost track of the days of the week lately.

The bar was crowded, with a mixed-together hum of noise hanging over it so thick you could almost see it. Most of the tables were full too, but I spotted an empty one off in a comer to the left of the doorway, which was just what I was wanting to see. I swiveled through the drinkers and the talkers and took a chair with the thick adobe wall secure and comforting at my back.

A waiter, a Mexican with a thick moustache and a spanking clean apron, took my order for a beer. When he brought it, he bumped a chair a few tables away and the man he'd jostled turned to look at him. It was Pepper

Watson, I was sure. One of the boys who'd made the drive with me.

"Pepper!" I hollered. "Hey, Pepper." He turned the rest of the way around and when he saw me hoisted his mug with a big smile. He jumped to his feet and nearly knocked the waiter over as he hurried to my table.

He thumped on my back, grinning and laughing the whole while. "By damn, Charlie. It's you for sure. We heard you was dead. Sure, am glad that ain't so. I sure am."

"Now that kinda tickles me too, Pepper, but how'd you get an idea like that? I've written to my folks several times in the past couple months. They should've gotten the letters all right."

He straddled a chair opposite mine and called for a refill on his beer. "Aw, I haven't been back to your part of the country since you paid us off. I guess that explains it then. But say, it's awful good to see you, Charlie. I ran into Bud Terry just the other day and he was telling me about it. Said he heard you was held up and shot dead on your way home from Kansas. Sure did. Won't he be surprised to learn he was wrong?"

"Yeah, I guess he will be," I said. I wondered if Terry could possibly have missed making the connection between me and the fellow he just had to know was looking for him. If he had heard just a description I supposed it was just barely possible he could still think he'd killed me. It seemed incredible, but still...

"Listen, Pepper. If you see Bud before I do, don't tell him you've seen me. I'd like to surprise him myself."

"Sure," Pepper said agreeably. The waiter came back.

Pepper took the fresh mug and immediately asked for another pair of them for us.

"What are you doing here anyway? And loaded with money to boot?"

"Say, Charlie. I really fell into a good thing. When we split up I headed back south. Got as far as Austin and met a fella driving beef west if you can believe that. So far, I've been on two drives for him, moving stockers across the river to the country just south of here. He's moving his whole operation into New Mexico. I've got a good job for the winter and come spring we'll bring some more over. It's a good deal, Charlie, so don't be looking for me when you sign your crew next year. I figure to be right here."

"I'm real happy for you, Pepper," I said. And I was. Pepper was a steady one, and if he'd found a year-round job it would be a good thing for him and for his boss too. He wasn't the kind who would let you down in big ways or in the little ones.

He sure seemed happy about everything, and I spent better than an hour sitting there with him, most of that time listening to him talk. When he finally began to run out of things to say he got quiet for a moment or two and then lit up with another of those big, open grins of his.

"Say, Charlie, why don't we ride out and see old Bud. I'd sure like to see the look on his face when he gets a peep at you."

"You know where he'd be now?"

"Sure," he said. "It's not more'n a half hour from here. How 'bout it?"

"Let's go," I said.

Pepper got his money down quicker than I could and

wouldn't listen to any argument about me paying any part of our bill. I didn't argue much. He was having himself a good time. And my mind was on other things just then.

Pepper was riding a yellow and white spotted horse that looked too small for him—he was not an extra big fellow either—but the animal had good bones and that quickness which usually makes a good cow pony. We headed west toward the higher ground off in the distance and inside of a few miles turned south into a dry, sparsely grassed narrow pocket.

A trail too narrow for a wagon twisted in and around some thick brush and around a mud patch that might have been a small pond at other times of the year. At the end of the track was a low roofed log building.

"Is this it?" I asked when we were in sight of it.

"Sure is," Pepper said over his shoulder. "Hold up a minute then, would you?"

He stopped, and I drew up beside him. I hemmed and hawed for a minute. I didn't want Pepper to think I'd been taking advantage of him. "Look," I said finally, "you might want to go back now. I mean, I don't want to be pulling any dirty tricks on you, Pepper. You see, the reason Bud was so sure I'd been robbed and killed is that he's the one did the robbing and the shooting. He just didn't quite manage to make it permanent."

"My Gawd, Charlie!" Pepper looked about as shocked as ever a man could. He puffed up red in the face and began to really bristle. "Anybody that'd ride with a man, eat his beef, take his pay an' then..." He sputtered to a halt. "Tell me about it."

So I did, leaving out only that it was Lee who'd sided Bud that time. When I was done Pepper had a tight, hard look to him. "There's three of them staying here," he told me. "Bud and a great big man called Jimmy and a greasy lookin' one called Ramon or Ray. Something like that. Let me carry that rifle off your saddle, an' we'll go talk to ol' Bud about this."

I shook my head. "That's little Jimmy Childress in there, Pepper, and another of his boys. They're purely killers. I cain't have you going up against the likes of them."

"Bull," he snapped. "That's all the more reason for you not to brace them by yourself." He reached across to the roan and lifted my rifle out of the boot. I went to say something to him, but he had already lifted his pony into a lope, heading straight for the front of that house. I had to either follow him or let him get into trouble alone.

Pepper reined up near the doorway and hollered, "Bud! Come out here, Bud." The door opened and a thin, dapper fellow who I'd never seen before stepped out. He seemed to recognize Pepper and did not appear to be alarmed, but he sure did look upset when Pepper leveled the muzzle of the rifle at him.

I got off the roan and slapped him on the hip to send him trotting a few yards away from me. I waved Pepper and the other man to the side. "Call him again," I told Pepper softly.

"Come out here a minute, Bud. You and Jimmy."

"Yo," a voice replied, muffled, from the house.

Bud and a tall, powerfully built man stepped into the sunlight. They were looking at Pepper as if he'd gone suddenly crazy. "What the hell is this about?" Childress demanded. He looked to be about as nasty as he was big.

"Over here, boys. We have some business, you and me."

CHAPTER 27

Bud looked as if he'd just been shot. Or seen a ghost, and I guess to him that was exactly what he was seeing. A dead man come back to haunt him. He went as pale as an egg shell, and he looked about as rigid and as brittle as one. Childress simply looked puzzled. "What is this?" he growled again.

"My name is McMurty, Mr. Childress, and I believe you have something that belongs to me." I was standing squared off toward them, feet slightly spread. Ready to explode.

Childress looked me up and down—Bud was in no condition for that; he just stared at me with this horrified expression on him—and then Little Jimmy Childress began to smile.

"You're the one," Childress said. "You been chasin' after me, shootin' my boys. You been bothering me, boy." He grinned happily. "I sure am glad to see you. Damn straight, I am." He took a step forward and conversationally mentioned, "I'm going to kill you now an' get you off my back, boy. You shouldn't ought to mess with me, you know."

"I'll mess with you as far as I have to, Mr. Childress," I told him. "What I came for is the money Bud took from me. Most of it belongs to my neighbors, and I figure to have it back. If you'd care to hand it over, I will go away and not bother you further. Otherwise I will have to take it back. But I intend to get it, regardless."

Childress stopped with a half dozen paces between us. He reached up with his right hand to tip his hat back, and he laughed and laughed. "That is a good one, boy. You are going to take money from Little Jimmy Childress. Oh, I like that. Did you hear that, Bud? Did you?"

He made as if to turn toward Bud, who was behind him, but only his head turned. His shoulders did not swing at all, and I was waiting for his hand to move.

It did, sweeping across his hip and lifting a heavy revolver deftly from its leather.

I'd already let my reflexes take over. The big Dragoon smacked solidly into my palm and bucked in recoil before I had time to consciously will the placement of the bullet. But I'd been looking at Childress' chest to take in any movement of his body, and that was where the first bullet went.

His gun went off, but he must have jerked the trigger by accident. I don't know where the bullet went. Childress looked slowly down at the hole in his chest, just beginning now to show a little blood. He shook his head. I believe he must have been dismissing the possibility of what he saw there. He re-cocked his revolver and raised it again.

I stepped to the side, trying now to watch Bud as much as Childress, and put a ball into Childress' forehead before he could swing his gun back in line with me. He dropped, apparently still not believing he could have been beaten.

Bud looked at him and seemed to snap out of the daze he'd been in. He started to take a step forward, faltered and brought his eyes up to meet mine. His face twisted, and he shook his head slowly from side to side. He reached with trembling fingers to fumble open the buckle of his gun belt, dropping it to the ground with his hands never coming near the revolver. I supposed it was the same one I'd had such a good look at before.

If Bud had prospered from his once-in-a-lifetime robbery opportunity it did not show. He did not look like a well man.

I glanced over at Pepper and the other man. I was really surprised to see Ramon or Ray or whoever he was stretched out on the ground in a pool of blood. I had never heard Pepper shoot, and those Winchesters make a bunch of noise.

"Charlie?" Bud's voice was weak, almost a whisper. "I have some of it left, Charlie. You can have it. Every bit of it. Honest. Every bit of it." He hurried inside the house.

Pepper ambled over to me. He seemed completely unconcerned by the turn of things although he had jumped from going on a friendly visit into a cloud of powder smoke. "I don't know that you oughta trust ol' Bud in there all alone," he said.

I sighed. "I don't know, Pepper. In a way I almost wish he would come out with a gun." But I didn't, really. I don't truly know just what I did feel then except for a dreary emptiness. There certainly was no sense of victory or great accomplishment. I thought there should have been.

Bud came stumbling back into the yard. He was carrying a pair of saddle bags instead of a gun. They looked familiar and then I realized why. They used to be mine.

"Here," he said. "It's all here. Everything I have left." He dug into one of the pockets and pulled out a thin sheaf of hundred-dollar bills. He pressed them into my hands.

Without thinking I began to count. Two thousand four hundred dollars. Twenty-four slips of paper. "That's all of it? This?"

Bud went pale all over again. "I swear. Every bit."

"You stole more than fifty thousand dollars from me. This can't be all of it."

"But... I swear, Charlie. I had ... I had to split. With Jimmy. And the boys. You know."

"And Lee?" I asked, forgetting for the moment that Pepper was listening.

"Well, you see, Charlie, he wasn't, well, he just wasn't the same. Afterward, I mean. An' Jimmy, he didn't trust the kid. Jimmy took his share, you see. But I had some friends of Jimmy's take care of him and promised to pay for what he needed. You can see that, can't you?"

"Yes, I guess I do see, Bud. What happened to the money Childress had?"

"I don't know. Honest I don't."

"Charlie," Pepper put in, "you used to wear a money belt." I looked at him. "Aw, it wasn't any secret from anybody. Not after all of us livin' together those months. Anyway, what I was getting at is, take a look under that fella's shirt," he said. He jerked a thumb toward Childress' body.

"You're experienced in that sort of thing, Bud. Bring it here."

"Sure, Charlie. Sure." He hurried to the body and knelt beside it, carefully staying away from the revolver Childress had dropped. He felt around Childress' waistline and gave me a ghastly smile of delight. If he still felt a reluctance to take money off a dead man he did not show it. He pulled the money belt free and brought it to me. It was my own belt, with some stains added to it since the last time I'd seen it. Fresh stains and some old ones that I could guess were put there by Bud Terry some months before.

The pockets of the belt were not nearly so lumpy as they had been. In all, including what Terry had had and what Pepper found in Childress' and Ramon's gear, there was a little over twenty-five thousand left.

"A lot of money but awful far short of what I owe," I said when it was all found and counted.

Pepper rubbed at his jaw. "There must be some flyers out on these boys," he said. "From what you've been telling me, you've picked up some of it that way. They could add a little to it. An' they were waiting here to meet someone. I heard them saying that the other day, Charlie. There might be some money on those fellas too."

"Yeah."

Oh, I could do that easy enough. Wait right there for whoever showed up. Go out and hunt down some more if they didn't bring in enough. Go on collecting bounty money for as long as it took. That sheriff, Kalb, he'd had enough bounty flyers on his wall to keep a man busy for a long, long time. And then go back to my Evie without a debt to drag us down. A lot of blood but no debts. It was real logical.

I grinned at Pepper and slapped him on the shoulder. "Pepper ol' hoss, if you can collect anything on that chilled beef lying around, you're welcome to it. That's only fair. As for me, I got some traveling to do."

"What about him?" Pepper pointed toward Bud Terry.

"You know, Pepper, I can't think of a single thing to do with him. He won't fight. And I guess I'm not much of a hand at murder. Guess I do better with cow critters than with the likes of him. But do you know something? I'm sorta glad to find that out. I really am."

"If you say so, Charlie."

"Do you know what I'm going to do, Pepper? I'm damn well going home. Right now. Today. I'm going home to that girl I left there."

"To Evelyn."

"How'd you know about her?"

"You prob'ly didn't talk about her more than twice a day, Charlie, the whole way from Texas to Kansas."

I hadn't realized that. "Well anyway, yeah. To my Evie."

"I sure don't envy you, Charlie. All that money owed. How much is it?"

"Something around ten thousand," I told him. I stuck out a hand. "Good luck to you, Pepper. And thank you."

We shook, ignoring Bud Terry who anyway seemed to

be trying to make himself invisible. "Good luck, Charlie," Pepper called after me.

Well, I figured to have it. I could borrow from my father to pay off the rest of my debt. Take a herd up next year. If I got an early enough start with that one, drive another one later the same season. One should pay off my dad. The second would be for Evie. And for a new saddle. I promised myself that. The first one hadn't been around here, but I could always get another. Next year.

In the meantime, well, who ever heard of a cowman anyway who wasn't in debt?

My fingers brushed the butt of the Dragoon there on my belly. On an impulse I stopped the roan and stood in the stirrups, so I could loosen my belt. I shoved the holster around, so it rode on my hip. One of these days I'd have to remember to cut a thong to hold the thing in place in the holster. If I got into a storm with a rank horse and a bad steer it might fall out. Someone might get hurt.

I felt a whole lot better when I bumped the horse in the ribs and put him into a slow lope. Toward Texas.

A LOOK AT LEAVING KANSAS (HARRISON WILKE BOOK 1)

BY FRANK RODERUS

Harrison Wilke is thoroughly sick of Redbluff, Kansas. The town is a boring dead end, filled with unlettered roughnecks. His uncle Stewart - from whom he stands to inherit the Running W Ranch - can't stand him. Harrison doesn't even have enough money to get to the big city, where he belongs. There are few bright spots.

Things begin to look up when Uncle Stewart turns up missing and feared dead while chasing rustlers. Then Harrison invests $4,000 in a very lucrative and secret deal. Of course Harrison "borrowed" the money from Uncle Stewart's safe. And Harrison also seems to be winning at love. But things do come crashing down....

AVAILABLE NOW

ABOUT THE AUTHOR

Frank wrote his first story—it was a western—when he was five. It was really awful, as might be expected, but his mother kept that typed and spell-checked short story tucked away until the day she died.

Later, Frank became a newspaper reporter, thinking that books are written by authors which he most assuredly was not. He kept trying to write though, and eventually did it wrong enough to learn how to get it right. That first sale, a young adult novel published by Independence Press, was more than thirty years and a good many books ago.

As a journalist, the Colorado Press Association awarded Frank their highest award, the Sweepstakes Award, for the best news story of 1980, and the Western Writers of America has twice named Frank recipient of their prestigious Spur Award. Frank passed away at age 73 in December 2015.